ANNA SPARROWS

A Stable Daddy

Down Under Daddies Book One

Cover design by Ky at Blue Brolli Graphics

Cover Photographer: Christopher John at CJC Photography

Cover Models: Kevin Davis & Brandon English

First edition

For anyone who has loved and lost.

(And an honorary shout out to Dixon Dallas, who will never read this, but whose song 'Something To Feel' was played on repeat for most of the time I spent writing this book. Especially during THAT scene. You'll know it when you get there.)

Contents

Preface

A Stable Daddy is a mostly sweet and fluffy Daddy kink (**without** age play) novel about two men learning to find love —and themselves— again. Inside you'll find a Texan cowboy putting down roots in Western Australia, a widower vet who might have always been someone's Boy without realising it, and the kinkiest and queerest band of stationhands any outback cattle station has ever seen.

*CW: Despite having one American MC, A Stable Daddy is written in Australian English (with Australian spelling). The book also contains impact play/spanking, choking/breath play, edging, and the use of a chastity cage, as well as themes of loss/grief (including the sudden death of a spouse), anxiety and self-doubt. **There is also a scene detailing on page mild sexual assault (a coerced BJ and deliberately ignoring a safe-word).***

For international readers, I've included a glossary of some of the Australianisms inside, but I'm a little worried I've missed a few:

Glossary (non-alphabetised because I'm a rebel):

Ute = pickup truck

You right? = Are you all right?

Ocker = can be used both as a noun and adjective for an Australian who speaks in a broad Australian accent and who acts in a rough/"country" sort of way

Bundy = Bundaberg (in the case of 'who gave him the Bundy?' It's referring to Bundaberg rum.)

Brissie = short for Brisbane

Stop being a sook = stop sulking

Woolies = Woolworths (a grocery store)

Yeah, nah = no

Nah, yeah = yes

Hatted Restaurant = a prestigiously awarded restaurant

Acknowledgments

First and foremost, let's all acknowledge how perfect Kevin Davis and Brandon English are on this cover. When I saw this photo, taken by Christopher at CJC Photography, it was beyond perfect for the story I had simmering away in my brain. Then Ky at Blue Brolli Graphics designed the gorgeous cover itself and *voila!* I am in love with the finished product. Thank you to everyone involved in bringing this cover to life.

Speaking of bringing the book to life, a HUGE thank you to Myf Wren for helping conceive the basic bones of this one. Without Myf, Wombat Run Station wouldn't have a name or a location. One day, I hope she will write her own Down Under Daddies book.

Also, thank you to Cindy, my alpha reader, for reading the first messy version of this novel and giving me valuable feedback to reshape it into a draft I was more than happy with. My beta readers, Erin, Megan, and MJ Booth helped polish that draft to the final version, and their feedback settled my nerves for putting forward something a little different to what I'm used to writing, so a big hug and thank you to each of them as well.

And, finally, thank you, the reader, for picking this book up. I know there are countless books out there you could have chosen, and it means a lot that you're offering my writing some of your time and attention in a world where time is a precious commodity. Even if you DNF (which is totally valid!), I appreciate the chance you've taken on me. (And if you want to talk about the book at all, please do feel free to email me or reach out to me on my socials. I love talking about books with people!)

Chapter One – Ryan

The club is packed. I'm not surprised, considering it's a Saturday night and a themed event night to boot. I've been visiting The Vault for years, but every time I climb the stairs that lead up from the well-stocked adult store beneath it, I feel the same thrill of nervousness creep up my spine.

Putting myself out there has never been my forte.

It was easier when I was married. Maddox and I were a team. A united front. I wasn't searching for a partner in the clubs, but rather celebrating and indulging my kinks with my husband in a safe, but still kind of public space. We'd come out to socialise with other kinky people and even if we'd sometimes play with others, I never felt the pressure to find other playmates because I had Maddy.

Then the bastard up and died on me, and I was suddenly a fifty-year-old widowed Sub with no clue how to proceed in life.

I'll admit the life choices I made in that first year were

questionable. I closed our (my) veterinary practice and sold our (my) house, unable to live with memories of Maddy etched into every nook and cranny. Then I moved back to Brisbane, where I'd grown up, and immediately missed the country.

But the one big thing Brisbane has that small rural towns don't? A thriving kink community…if you know where to look.

So, after rambling around a shoebox apartment for a couple of months, I bit the bullet and started researching the best clubs to visit. It was hit and miss at first, and the first Dom I did a scene with used his safe-word when the grief of missing Maddy hit me out of nowhere, but I eventually found The Vault hidden in the seedier area of Fortitude Valley, and I've been coming here ever since.

Usually on a night like tonight, when the club has arranged a ticketed themed event, I try to make plans with a Dom ahead of time. But my choice to come here was very last minute, and that makes me even more anxious about being on my own.

The space at the top of the stairs is dimly lit. It's a much larger area than the shop downstairs would have you believe. There's a large central room, with a projector screen showing porn on the right-hand wall, and a queen-sized bed right in front of it. White leather couches line the other walls, well placed to watch either the porn or any couples willing to play in front of an audience. There are a couple of stripper poles between the bed and the couches, too.

Beyond this room lies a catacomb of smaller rooms: some for playtime, some for more intimate porn viewing sessions. There's also an alcove containing a sex swing and a St Andrews cross, and at the very end of one of the hallways, a room for age play enthusiasts, complete with an adult sized crib and change table.

All in all, even though The Vault isn't the fanciest or largest club I've ever been to, it is well-appointed and the clientele are usually respectful of the club's rules.

However, tonight there's a strange vibe in the air. I don't know if I'm just projecting my anxiety, or whether it's the sheer number of bodies writhing under the dim lighting, but I feel on edge as I enter the main space.

I can feel eyes trailing over me, taking in my gold lamé shorts and white mesh tank top. Around my neck, I wear a collar of fluorescent blue glow sticks, and I have a matching bracelet on either wrist. I look like the 90s chewed me up and spat me back out, but that was tonight's theme, so I'm happy with my ensemble.

Well, I *was*. Now that I'm here, I'm second guessing all of my life choices.

Not many other people appear to have gone as gung-ho on matching the event theme. A few are wearing similar glow stick combinations to me, some wearing glow stick crowns or necklaces, but most people are in "normal" club clothes. Not booty shorts that were essentially stolen from a Kylie Minogue video.

"Oh, honey," a young, flamboyant Asian guy approaches me, his lip curled in amusement, "you went all out, didn't you?"

I sigh and accept his hug when he opens his arms wide, exchanging kisses to each other's cheeks. "Hey, Jake. What gives? I thought everyone was dressing up tonight?"

He snorts and points at his ripped jeans and black t-shirt combination. "I went nineties grunge, darling."

It takes every ounce of control I possess not to close my eyes and groan. "Of course you did."

He tosses his head back and laughs, making his Adam's apple bob. "You're adorable, Rye."

I screw my nose up. I might be submissive by nature, but I don't think I'm comfortable with my young friend calling me adorable. I'm twice his age, for one thing, and more silver fox than cutesy club bunny. Jake takes one look at my expression and snorts.

"You're really haggling for a paddling tonight, huh?" he asks.

"That's not a saying."

"Next you'll be telling me to stop trying to make fetch happen," he winks.

"God save me from ridiculous young brats," I roll my eyes towards the ceiling, but I'm unable to prevent the upwards twitch of my lips behind my salt and pepper goatee.

Jake hip checks me and I follow him through the crowd of people, nodding at a few I recognise, but realising that the majority are new faces. It's strange, considering the community itself is somewhat underground, and The Vault is one of the smaller clubs in the vicinity of the city.

"Frank advertised tonight's event on Red Hot Pie," Jake rises up on his toes so he can speak the words directly into my ear. The fact that his warm breath ghosting over my skin makes me shudder is a sign that it's been way too long since I last played with anyone. "The store's been struggling. He thought getting fresh blood in might help revive it a bit."

Nodding in understanding, my heart goes out to Frank and Antonia. They own the adult store downstairs as well as the club itself, and they've become good friends over the past year or so. It sucks to hear that the business isn't doing well.

"Hopefully the plan pays off for them," I muse, allowing my eyes to drift past the bed, where two men are worshipping a curvaceous brunette between them, to the wall where the porn is playing. It's het porn tonight, which doesn't surprise me. One of the smaller, private viewing rooms will be showing gay porn.

Still, I can appreciate the sight of the large spit slicked cock currently pistoning in and out of cherry red lips on the projector screen.

"I hope so, too," my friend agrees, "it would suck if they had to close."

Even though the contract I signed three weeks ago means I won't be able to be a regular anymore, the thought of never being able to visit my friends in the community in our favourite hangout makes my stomach twist and churn with anxiety.

"Yeah," I agree solemnly, "it would."

We lean against a wall near the occupied couches and chat quietly as we watch people interacting. I've already spotted a couple of promising looking Doms, assuming they're willing to play with another man. I know I could always find Lisa and beg her to strap me to the cross and lash my back the way I know she enjoys the most, but I'd much prefer a man to take control tonight and push me over the edge of orgasm. I'm antsy and I need sexual release as well as the endorphins of subspace.

One of the new Doms catches me watching him as he slowly wraps a rope bunny in a complicated shibari pattern. I'm mesmerised by how sensual and methodical his movements are, and how beautifully they move together as she anticipates every strap and twist of the silky looking rope.

Once she's fully trussed, completely naked bar for the criss-crossing emerald pattern over her beautiful Black skin, I watch him bend her over. He threads the fingers of one hand through a section of rope on her back and tugs her until she's arching back to meet him. With his free hand, he pulls a condom from his pocket, tears the foil square open with his teeth, then rolls the latex sheath over his rigid cock, locking his eyes with mine as he sinks inside his play partner.

He forces her to hold her pose as he fucks her slowly, but my attention is focused solely on him. She cries out her release and bucks in his hold, and his eyes shift from mine as he releases the rope to grab at her hips and fuck her with wild abandon.

It's that wildness which makes my cock stir to life. I want that sort of energy directed my way.

And so, after they've finished and cleaned up, and he has presumably taken her into one of the quiet rooms for some aftercare, I seek him out.

"Wanna play?" he asks me, cocking his head to the side as we stand facing each other in a quiet hallway, rows of doors on either side of us. Muted moans and sounds of others enjoying themselves occasionally filter out, but I don't pay them any mind.

I nod. "I'd like that, yeah."

He makes a show of looking me up and down. I try not to fidget beneath the appraisal. I know I look ridiculous in what I'm wearing, and I'm at least a decade older than him, too. But I need this tonight. "Limits?" he asks.

"I don't do humiliation," I tell him, quirking my lips into a self-deprecating smile. "Well, no more than wearing this outfit out tonight." He snorts, and I feel the tension in my shoulders loosen. "No CNC, no watersports, no scat play. Also, my knees aren't what they used to be, so I can't kneel for extended periods of time." I cock my head. "You?"

The Dom nods contemplatively. "I can work with that."

I frown a little, not liking that he avoided the question, but the desperation to submit and find subspace pushes me onwards. "Standard traffic light safe-words?"

He shakes his head. "If you're going to safeword, I want to hear you say 'Grenade'."

I bite my lip. It's certainly not a word I would casually drop into conversation, but I don't love it. Nevertheless, I can't think of a reason not to agree. "Okay," I tell him. "Where do you want me?"

I follow him into one of the private rooms, which is small to the point of feeling cramped. It's the size of a glorified storage cupboard, containing a plastic seat and not much else.

"I want you to undo my pants, get on your knees and suck my cock," he demands, and I hesitate.

I did just tell him that I can't be on my knees for long, but I suppose I didn't tell him that it was completely off the table, so I can only hope that this won't be a long session on the floor.

"Yes, Sir," I answer when my hesitation goes on for just a touch too long. Then I do as he's requested, unbuckling his belt and hitching his jeans down before I sink to my knees in front of him.

"Condom?" I ask him, confident with my question considering the fact that I watched him use one earlier.

He shakes his head. "I'm negative."

"I'd be more comfortable if—"

"Do you want to play or not?" he snaps.

I swallow roughly.

I should use my safe-word. I should walk away. My instincts are telling me I'm making the wrong decision by not following through.

But I'm older than most of the people here tonight, and the

majority have paired up already anyway. If I don't seize this opportunity to be dominated, there's every chance I'll leave the club even more frustrated and caught up in my head than when I arrived.

With my heart hammering, I open my mouth and he thrusts into it without warning, his fingers sinking into the greying hair on my head, gripping and tugging it painfully. Tears spring to my eyes, caused both by the rough treatment and by my instant regret.

There's submission and then there's this.

This doesn't feel right.

I tap on his thigh, realizing too late that with my mouth full, I can't speak the safe-word.

He ignores my efforts.

Not for the first time tonight, I'm overwhelmed by how badly I miss Maddy. My sweet, patient Dom. He'd been ruthless when necessary, but he'd always known what I needed and how I needed it. I'm still making mistakes without his guidance.

The tears in my eyes spill over and I hit this guy's thigh a little harder.

"Fuck," he stops thrusting and yanks my head backwards, any sign of the meticulous man who had slowly wrapped a woman in rope earlier in the evening completely vanished. *"What?"* he spits at me.

"Gr-grenade," I stammer, and his eyes go wide with disbelief.

"The fuck?" he demands, yanking my head harder.

"Grenade," I repeat, louder this time. "Red light."

"You're a fucking cock tease," he complains angrily, and I flinch back.

"Please, let my hair go," I request, feeling my whole body start to tremble.

I've never come across a situation like this before, and I'm realising too late that I've been careless. I should have told Jake where I was going. I shouldn't have gone into a private, closed-door room with someone I've never played with before. I should have backed out when the warning bells first started ringing in my mind.

"You're going to finish me off first," he says. "It's the least you can do."

I gape up at him, my knees starting to twinge with pain. But that's the least of my concerns.

Fifty-one-fucking-years-old, and I'm about to become (or have I already become?) a victim of sexual assault.

"I said no," I raise my voice, hoping that the sound might carry into the hall. I know the number one club rule is to never open a closed door, but maybe someone will break it if they can hear that I'm in genuine distress. "I safeworded!"

I should have anticipated the slap, but it takes me by surprise.

My cheek stings and my eyes water all over again as my face snaps to the side. The movement, though, brings me hope. Through blurry vision, I can see that the door is open a crack. I lunge sideways for it, managing to slip my fingers into the crack between the door and the doorway, slamming the whole thing open with as much force as I can muster while my would-be (actual?) assailant trips over his own pants.

"Help!" I call out, trying to scramble back to my feet despite my stiff, protesting knees. "Red light! Help! Anyone?!"

"How dare you?!" the guy behind me demands, and I feel his fingers take a handful of the mesh at my back, tugging me backwards.

I stumble, falling in his direction, hoping that he'll break my landing.

A Stable Daddy

This was not how I imagined tonight going at all.

Chapter Two – Oscar

I've done a hell of a lot of dumb shit in my life, but moving halfway around the world for some guy I met on the internet is probably the dumbest shit of all.

Especially when I found out he had a wife.

And kids.

And a cute-as-fuck dog.

I sure as shit wasn't turning back around and hopping on another long-haul flight back to Texas. Not to hear my mama bitching me out about how she told me so, or to hear my pops telling me that if I'd just lived my life the way they'd told me to, none of this would have happened.

I've forever been a disappointment to them. And, the more they expressed those thoughts, the more I rebelled. That accounts for maybe sixty percent of my shitty decisions. The other forty percent? That's all on me.

So here I am in Brisbane, Australia, of all places, having just checked myself in to a hotel in the city and looking to let off a bit of steam before I make a plan to get my life back on track…again.

The central business district of the city feels small. It kind of reminds me of the time I visited San Diego as a kid. Could probably walk from one end of the place to the other within a couple of hours if I tried. Hell, it feels like you could take the whole area and drop it in the middle of my pop's ranch and still have acres upon acres of land to spare.

But then, they do say everything's bigger in Texas.

I pull out my phone and, using the sim card I'd organised myself when I'd planned to uproot my entire life, I start searching for my usual kinds of stress-relief.

I scroll a few online message boards before I find the advertisement for a kink-friendly club called 'The Vault'. A quick Google search tells me it's only a mile and a half's walk from my hotel, and apparently they're still selling tickets for tonight's themed event.

I ain't planning on going in costume, and I'm willing to bet they'll let me in regardless. So, after tucking my phone and wallet into my pockets, I head out the door and in the direction of the club.

* * *

The club, like Brisbane City, is smaller than I imagined it would be. I almost couldn't find the damn place to start with, not realising that it was part of the adult store I'd walked past three times. With its peeling pink exterior and grimy windows, it wasn't exactly an enticing place to walk into, but the interior was bright and squeaky clean, and the woman behind the counter was more than happy to direct me up the stairs to the club after I showed her the ticket on my phone.

Beyond the soundproofed door at the top of the stairwell, the sounds and sights hit me all at once. Writhing bodies, moans and groans, slaps and slurps and general debauchery. Even if it is a much smaller, more dated space than I'm used to back home, it's still familiar and comforting.

I explore the space first, respecting the closed-door rule wherever I come across one, but poking my head into rooms with open doors, watching the porn and live shows for a few moments before moving on. I'm just trying to get a feel for the space and the kind of activities I'm in the mood for when sounds of distress filter down one of the short hallways lined with closely spaced-together doors.

I pause and wait, wondering if it's part of someone's play, or whether the distress is real.

I jump a few seconds later when the sound of a door slamming against a wall reaches me, dim yellow light spilling out into the hall from the fourth door on the left.

"Help!" A guy's voice, pitched high with panic calls out, "Red light! Help! Anyone?!"

My legs are moving before my brain catches up with my intentions.

When I reach the open doorway, it's to the sight of some bland, dark-haired guy wearing a rumpled button-down shirt and dark denim jeans around his ankles grabbing a terrified looking man by the back of his mesh shirt and pulling him so hard that they both topple backwards.

The older man cries out and flails his arms, shutting his eyes as he falls.

Launching forward, I manage to grasp his wrist, pulling him towards me.

His blue-grey eyes fly open as he tries to lean into my

movement, crying out again when the mesh of his shirt tears and his attacker crashes backwards to the ground. The sudden release sends the guy I'm rescuing careening into me.

I stagger, but manage to twist us enough that my back hits the wall and stops our momentum. The man against me is trembling and I don't hesitate to wrap my arms around him. His skin is warm to the touch, and he takes the contact as an invitation to burrow his bearded face into the crook of my neck, his breathing heavy and hitching.

"You're okay," I soothe. "I've got you."

He nods but doesn't speak, and I glare over in the direction where the other guy is picking himself up off the floor. "What happened here?"

"You broke a club rule," the other guy snaps at me. "Fuckin' Americans, always thinking you own the world. You can't just bust in on someone's scene."

"I didn't break anything," I keep my tone calm as I reply, aware that the raised voice of the other guy made the man in my arms flinch. I tilt my head towards the hallway. "That door was wide open, and it sounded to me as though you were the one breaking club rules."

All my response earns me from the asshole is a sneer. "Fuck off. We were just—"

"Was this man safewording?" I cut him off, absently rubbing calming circles on the older man's back when he attempts to burrow even deeper into the crease between my shoulder and neck.

"It was part of the scene," the asshole says flippantly.

I frown; an expression which deepens as the man in my arms shakes his head against me. "That true, darlin'?" I ask him, holding an index finger up to silence the protests from the mouthy guy in the corner.

"No." The word is barely whispered, but with how close his mouth is to my ear, I hear it loud and clear.

"Oh, come *on*," the asshole whines, gesturing wildly towards us, "look at the way he's dressed. He was begging for it."

The man in my arm whimpers and I decide I've heard and seen enough. "I'm gonna go ahead and call bullshit on that, buddy." I tell the guy in the corner, giving the one in my arms a reassuring squeeze. "And you're gonna stay right here while I report this to the insanely huge security guy I was introduced to earlier."

That announcement goes down like a lead balloon, and the asshole yells as he tells me I ain't got no right to report him or whatever. I tune him out, my protective instincts kicking into gear as every loud exclamation earns another shudder from the man in my hold.

"What's going on here?" The new voice belongs to the aforementioned security guy. He stands in the still open doorway, his arms folded and his expression menacing.

I can see there's a crowd growing behind him, and I smother a sigh. An audience is the last thing the man I've stepped in to assist needs.

"This guy," the asshole cries dramatically, waving his hand at me, "*burst* into this room while *that* guy and I were in the middle of a scene and—"

"The door was open," I object calmly, "and he was safewording and calling out for help."

"It was part of the scene," the asshole insists, taking on a tone that suggests he thinks I'm a moron.

I raise my eyes towards the ceiling and silently ask The Powers That Be to grant me strength.

The security guy, big and hulking, looks between us with narrowed eyes before his gaze lands on my charge. Immediately, his dark eyes widen with recognition.

"Rye?" he asks in disbelief.

Rye, for his part, pulls away from my neck to peek in the security guy's direction. I catch a glimpse of tear tracks on his cheek, and I have to count backwards from ten in my head to not push him into the security guy's arms just so I can go and pummel the crap out of the sorry excuse of a man in the corner of the room.

"Well, shit." The security guy breathes. He doesn't ask any further questions. Instead, he pushes forward into the room, bypassing me and Rye, and takes the asshole by the bicep. He looks back over at us. "I'm taking him downstairs. We've got his details and he will be banned from the store and the club. But, Ryan, if he crossed a line —if he tried to force you— you're within your rights for us to call the police and make a report." He says all of this kindly. His grip tightening on the other man's arm while the guy struggles is the only sign that he's clearly just as pissed as I am. Maybe even more, seeing as he knows the man in my arms well enough to be on a first-name basis with him.

Ryan pulls back again, shaking his head. He swallows roughly. "I don't want to do that. Just...just take him away. Please, Sam?"

The asshole cusses and curses and protests the whole way out the door. I ignore the murmur of conversation from the hallway, gently holding Ryan by the shoulders as I ask, "Do you want to go into another room and take a minute? I totally get it if being alone with a strange Dom after all that doesn't work for you, but I'd like to get you out of this room and I'm bettin' you'd like to avoid the crowd out there." I remove my hands when it hits me that my touching him might also be making him uncomfortable, and I facepalm. "I'm Oscar, by the way."

Ryan is already shaking his head, in what I assume is refusal of my offer. "No," he says softly, then forces himself to look me in the eye. He looks a mess with his silver-streaked hair dishevelled and his eyes red-rimmed, but I'm not unaware of how attractive he is. "No, I…I'd like it if we took a minute." Beneath his neatly trimmed goatee, which is greyer than the dark hair on top of his head, his lips curl into a small smile. "I'm Ryan."

I hold out my hand to shake his. "It's a pleasure to meet you, Ryan," I tell him, then cringe again. "Maybe not under these circumstances, but I'm always happy to make the acquaintance of a handsome man."

His face flushes pink and it's damned adorable. "Now you're just being nice to make me feel better."

I snort. "Darlin', I'm not the kind of man who lies about things like that. If I say you're handsome, it's because I think you are."

The Adam's apple in his throat bobs and he bites his lip. "Okay. Thank you." After a beat, he adds, "You are, too. Handsome, I mean."

It's cute the way his cheeks flush and he looks to the floor. I don't think he's complimenting me for the sake of returning the gesture, not by his suddenly shy and awkward demeanour. It's pressing all of my buttons right now, and I have to remind myself that he's been through an ordeal and doesn't need a horny cowboy pawing at him. He needs a friend, even if only for the night.

"Come on, sweetheart," I press my hand to the small of his

back to lead him from the room and then frown as my open palm makes contact with bare flesh. "On second thought, hold up."

"What…?" he starts to ask, his eyes widening as I tug my leather jacket off, exposing my short-sleeved shirt and my heavily tattooed arms.

The jacket is well-worn and buttery soft. Brown, not black, and the lining is silky smooth satin.

I hold it out to him with a smile.

"You're about the same size as me, I'm guessin'. This'll be better than that scrap you're stuck with right now. Here," I right the upturned chair and lay my jacket over it, turning back to Ryan, my hands reaching for what remains of his 'shirt'. "Let me?"

The pink shade over the tops of his cheeks deepens, but he allows me to assist him out of the mess of mesh he'd been wearing. Then I help him into my jacket, and I'm pleased to find that it's a close fit, if slightly too big around the shoulders. A pang of *something* hits me at seeing him in my clothes. Something undefinable, but nonetheless warm and fuzzy. It's not quite possessive, but it makes me feel like he's mine.

That is dangerous.

I'm on the rebound, I have to acknowledge that. I'm also being presented with all of my favourite temptations at once: a sweet, shy older man, submissive to the core, *and* he just let me dress him. As a Daddy Dom, I'm aching to see what else we could do together.

But those same Daddy instincts have me backing off, too. I'm feeling protective and I want to offer comfort, and those are the only lines I'll cross with him.

That ain't gonna stop me from daydreaming, though.

Chapter Three — Ryan

I'm surprised when the room Oscar leads me into is the club's Nursery room. Surprised, but not uncomfortable. Especially when he sits me on the plush two-seater couch and then gestures to the door. "Open or shut?" he asks me. "Your call, darlin'."

Oh dear God, that accent.

As a kid, I used to watch spaghetti Westerns on TV, and I had a real fascination with American cowboys for a good portion of my youth. And even though the tattoos on this young man's arms, hands, and neck don't necessarily scream cowboy, everything else about him does.

So, suddenly, my old fascination is back.

I'm a city boy, born and raised in the suburbs of urban Australia. My accent isn't as thick and ocker as those who live out bush, but it still feels clunky and decidedly unsexy next to Oscar's. Or at least it does in my head.

"Closed, please," I answer, and he gives me a smile so warm that it makes my stomach flip pleasantly.

"I do like a Boy with manners," he teases as he shuts the door, and I snort.

"It's been a long time since anyone called me a boy."

Amusement lights up his eyes, which I finally notice are a golden kind of brown, like a well-aged whiskey, tiny gold highlights glinting in them when the yellow from the ceiling light hits them just right.

"Oh, honey," he says, grinning and shaking his head, "a man can be a Boy at any age." He gestures around the room and my answering smile slips a little as realisation dawns.

Oh.

"Oh," I repeat my stellar thought out loud. Then I swallow and look around again, taking in the change table and crib with a whole new understanding. "You meant Boy. With a capital 'b.'" I clasp my hands in my lap and fiddle with my fingers, suddenly nervous. "I've never…I mean, I'm not…Not that there's anything wrong with…" I stop my rambling, closing my eyes to take a deep, steadying breath. "I'm not a Boy. Just a sub."

"I know, darlin'." That voice of his is so very seductive. It's mellow and affectionate, but there's that sense of authority belying it which I have never been able to pin down or replicate. He's definitely a Dom, that's for sure.

"But…you're a Daddy?" The question tumbles from my lips before my brain to mouth filter can engage.

He nods, still wearing that gentle smile. "I am, yeah. But I'm also a Dom. I don't need my subs to regress if that's not somethin' they enjoy. But," he shrugs, and I watch the thin cotton of his black button-down shirt tighten around his biceps, "I don't like bein' called Master or Sir. It's Daddy or bust, I'm afraid."

A nervous giggle bubbles up from my stomach and I have to clear my throat to prevent it from escaping. "Y-you want me to call you Daddy?"

Oscar visibly startles at the question. "Oh! No. No, honey. I didn't bring you in here for a scene. I'd never do that without proper negotiation first. I just wanted to get you somewhere quiet and private, and this room was empty when I checked by earlier. I get the feelin' not too many people who visit this club are into this kind of play."

I should feel relief at his answer, but instead I'm surprised to feel a bubble of disappointment lodge itself in my chest. I rub at it, blinking when my hand encounters my chest hair. I look down and remember that I'm shirtless beneath my borrowed jacket. A jacket which smells like him, all spicy and warm.

"What's wrong?" he asks, and I firm my lips, shaking my head, prepared to refute him. But he snorts and continues, "I mean, aside from the obvious. I can be a real idiot sometimes, I swear."

"No, no, I'm…I'm okay," I assure him. "I mean, I'm a bit shaken up, but you got there before anything could happen." My throat works convulsively. "Thank you for that, by the way."

I was genuinely terrified that nobody would hear me. That nobody would come to my rescue.

"Hey now," Oscar inches closer, treating me like a flighty wild animal. He sits carefully on the mattress beside me and wraps an arm around my shoulders. I lean into his embrace, closing my eyes and enjoying the smooth cadence of his accent. "I didn't do anythin' special. I was just in the right place at the right time."

"You stopped him from forcing me…" My whole body

shudders. I was violated, had my safe-words ignored, and I was physically attacked…but I was rescued before my attacker could take things further, and I take solace in that.

"Are you sure you don't want to press charges, darlin'?" There's a hard edge to Oscar's voice now, but I know it's an anger directed at that other Dom and not at me.

I shake my head. "No, he didn't—"

"He still assaulted you." He keeps his tone gentle, and he gives me a little squeeze, which feels both apologetic and bracing. "I know you don't want to hear it, Ryan, but what he did *was* assault. And, before you try and tell me that it could have been worse, I want you to think about what kind of advice you'd give a friend if they said someone did to them what that man did to you, okay?"

Well, damn it.

"I hate it when people use logic on me," I grumble sulkily, but the corners of my lips pull upwards as he chuckles. Then I sigh and acknowledge, "If he'd pulled what he did on Jake or any of the other Subs, I'd tell them it was assault and that they should report it." Tears clog my throat and blur my vision. "I…I feel so stupid."

"No, baby, you're not stupid." His tone is firm. "This club is supposed to be a safe space. That sorry excuse for a man took advantage. He's the stupid one, not you."

"He's probably long gone," I shrug, still trying to blink away the tears.

"Except his ID is in the system downstairs. I had to hand over my passport to be let in, 'cause I ain't got my driver's licence here yet. But I know they took my details before I came on up here, and they woulda' done the same with him."

Gnawing on my bottom lip, I acknowledge that he's right

about that, too.

"I can come with you to the station if you'd like," he offers gently, and I'm overwhelmed by how sweet and kind an offer that is. "In fact," he continues, "I probably should, in case they need a witness statement. I won't be in the city for long, but I'll give them a way to contact me once I'm gone."

And that's how I wind up sitting in the Fortitude Valley Police Beat shopfront, making a report to a very friendly and understanding police officer.

Located in the middle of Brunswick Street, amongst the pubs and nightclubs, the space is brightly lit and exists as a stop-measure between all the craziness that happens in the city and the main police station, which is a short drive away. I'm willing to bet that they mostly deal with drunken shenanigans, but the officer who takes down my story and hands me information for counselling isn't at all judgemental. She hadn't even raised her eyebrows when I walked in wearing my booty shorts and Oscar's leather jacket and nothing else.

"For now, this report will be passed on to an investigator. They'll probably want to talk to you themselves, too. Then, they'll investigate," she assures me, speaking with compassion that seems completely genuine as I stand to leave, "and someone will be in touch."

I frown, "I'll be moving out of state in a couple of weeks. Will that be a problem?"

"Only if this goes to court. You may need to come back for that. But we'll take it one step at a time, okay? Just remember that you have choices through all of this, and you can ask for extra support through it, too."

Nodding, I shake her hand and she tells Oscar to make sure I get home safely, assuming that we're closer than we are. Before

I can protest, he assures her that he will, and then he guides me back out onto the main hustle and bustle of Brunswick Street with a firm hand on the base of my spine. I imagine I can feel the warmth of his palm through the leather, and I briefly wish that I wasn't wearing the jacket because I really like feeling his touch.

"Now, do you need me to call you an Uber or a cab? Or did you want to go back to the club, or…" he hesitates for half a second, "did you want to come back to my hotel room? Not for anything sexual," he's quick to add, "but it's nearby and, forgive me for sayin' this, darlin', but you look beat."

I wait for the voice of reason in my head to tell me that going to a strange Dom's hotel room is an even worse idea than going into a private room in the club, but that voice is silent. Oscar rescued me from that other guy. He's been nothing but gentle and courteous and hyper respectful of my potential boundaries. He even took me to make a police report and stuck around while I did. I feel like he's trustworthy, and he's right: I really am exhausted.

"If…if it's okay…I'd like that. To go back to your place. *Only* if it's really okay."

His handsome face lights up with the warmest smile I've seen him wear all night. "I'd like that, too, honey."

* * *

His hotel room is only a fifteen-minute walk from Brunswick Street. It's in one of the newer hotels, on the thirty-second floor and with a phenomenal view of the city's twinkling lights. The room is only a studio, though, with a king-sized bed, a tiny two-seater couch, and a very tiny kitchenette containing little more than a kettle, mini-fridge and sink. The bathroom is just as minimalistic, with a shower, toilet, and a tiny basin crammed into a space not much bigger than my walk-in wardrobe at home.

"I did not think this through," he muses sheepishly as he looks from the bed to the too-tiny couch, to me and then back to the bed. "I'm gonna take the floor, okay?"

"Absolutely not," crossing my arms, I glower at him. "This is your hotel room. I can still get an Uber home."

Disappointment flashes in his eyes and it warms me all the way to my toes.

"Or," I add, suddenly feeling shy and unsure of myself, "we can share the bed."

Heat flares in place of the disappointment before his cheeks flush and he blinks the lusty expression away. "I warn you," he points an index finger at me, "I'm respectful when I'm awake, but I'm a snuggler in my sleep."

The declaration makes my heart thud painfully in my chest. This beautiful young man reminds me so much of Maddy, despite looking nothing like him. It's in the way he wears his heart on his sleeve. The way he's determined to be honest and respectful at all times, but while still having that firm, dominant air about him.

When it comes to personalities, I've got a type, and this guy? He's everything I've ever been attracted to, if in a much younger package.

And he's only here temporarily, I remind myself. *Also, you're leaving in a couple of weeks, too.*

Not wanting to acknowledge why those thoughts hurt so much, I force a grin. "I like being cuddled."

"Is that so?" I don't know if I imagine the way his eyes light up, because he clears his throat and gestures to his suitcase sitting open on the coffee table in front of the little couch. "Anyway, let's get you into somethin' more comfortable, hmm?"

I'm loathe to let go of the leather jacket, and I'm also embarrassed to have to borrow his clothes at all. "I can just sleep in the shorts…"

A strangled sound comes from the vicinity of the back of his throat. "Darlin', you in just those shorts could tempt a priest to sin."

"Please," I scoff, looking down at myself. With the jacket open, my aging torso makes me feel vulnerable. I've been trying to keep myself fit, but my skin is still softening and wrinkling, marked with age spots and grey hairs. The six pack of my youth is gone, the toning to my belly even harder to maintain now than it was a year or two ago. "I've got one foot in the grave."

Pausing in his rummage through his clothes, Oscar looks up at me sharply. "I beg your pardon?"

"I appreciate how kind you've been, but I'm not unaware of my appearance. I'm old. Definitely too old for you. I…" the words I planned to say vanish from the tip of my tongue at the shift in energy in the room.

Oscar's expression is serious, but nothing about his demeanour scares me. Even though he's frowning at me, I don't feel the unease I felt with the other guy in the club.

"You don't get to tell me you're too old for me," he says slowly and deliberately. "Unless my being thirty-four is a problem for you—"

"Thirty-four?" He's seventeen years my junior. That thought makes me feel like a lecherous old man. "I'm old enough to be your father."

"Funny, because *I'm* the one who likes being called Daddy," he jokes, then cocks his head. "You're, what, forty-five? Fifty at a stretch?"

"Fifty-one," I sigh heavily and sit on the couch. "Almost fifty-two."

"Still a bit young to be my pops, but I suppose you're technically right." Then he shakes his head. "Not that age matters to me. I like older men. Especially when you've got that silver fox goodness goin' on." Lips quirking, he admits, "Maybe it's *my* daddy issues that got me wantin' to dominate older guys. I don't know, and I don't really care. As long as we're both consenting adults, age ain't nothin' but numbers."

I get a thrill at the way he casually admits he wants to dominate older guys, but before I can tell him I'd like to play, Oscar starts rummaging through his suitcase again. The clothes inside are all rolled into tight bundles, neatly arranged in rows. He obviously values order and tidiness, which I appreciate.

"These should work," he pulls out two bundles of soft cotton then shakes them out one by one. Navy cotton boxer shorts and a light blue t-shirt are extended my way. "Bathroom's through there," he gestures at the room I spied earlier, "and the hotel has complimentary toothbrushes."

I'm hit with a wave of loss as I carefully take the jacket off, handing it to him in exchange for the borrowed sleep clothes. When I'm out of his line of sight, I lift the t-shirt to my nose and sniff it. It's clean and fresh, smelling like it's been freshly laundered. Usually, I love the smell of freshly cleaned cotton, but it doesn't compare to the spicy, masculine scent trapped in the fibres of his jacket.

I get changed slowly, grimacing at the almost plastic *thwack* of lamé hitting glossy white tiles when I drop my boy shorts to the ground. My fingers hesitate before I reach for the cotton boxer shorts, but I drop those, too, when a knock sounds at the door.

"You doin' okay, darlin'?" Oscar asks, and my pulse skyrockets.

"Y-yeah," I answer, feeling decidedly off-kilter, but unable to explain why. "I'm just slow."

There's a brief moment of silence before he asks, "Would you like some help?"

I'm an adult. Have been one for a hell of a lot longer than he has, in fact. But for some strange reason, the idea of him helping me get dressed is appealing in ways I can't articulate. My mouth goes dry and my heart continues to pound rapidly in my chest.

"Darlin'?" he prompts, then, in a more serious tone, says, "Ryan?"

Looking at the puddles of fabric on the ground, I nibble my bottom lip for a moment before answering, "Help me?"

Chapter Four – Oscar

What can I say? I'm a sucker for a sweet Boy in need of assistance. I spring into action the second Ryan's plaintive plea reaches my ears, opening the door to find him standing in the middle of the small bathroom, naked and wide-eyed.

If you were to look up the definition of 'temptation' in my dictionary, this tableau would be pictured there.

Now, I know he's not a Boy, but I slip into Daddy-mode without a second's thought. Crossing the threshold, I stoop to pick up the boxer shorts I'm lending him for the night, then I kneel in front of him holding the waistband stretched open in invitation.

"Step in, honey," I instruct him, "one leg at a time."

A blush travels up his chest and neck and onto his face, but he does as I've asked. Then he stands still as I pull the shorts up his hairy legs, running my index fingers inside the elastic waistband once I have the shorts settled comfortably on his hips. I'm proud of myself for keeping my eyes on his the entire time, watching for discomfort, rather than allowing myself to be drawn to the delicious cock which is slowly filling and tenting the thin cotton now concealing it.

I push to my feet and smile at him. "Good boy," I praise and when he ducks his chin and his cheeks turn a deeper shade of pink, my stomach flips pleasantly. "Shirt now, okay?"

He nods and bites his lip. "Nuh-uh," I reach out and, using my thumb, gently pry the abused flesh from between his teeth. "We use our words, darlin'."

Adam's apple bobbing, Ryan hesitantly replies, "Yes…Daddy."

Holy shit, I should have braced for impact.

Nothing could have prepared me for the way it feels to hear him cautiously testing the title out in his cute-as-fuck Australian accent. Then I remind myself how new this is for him. "You don't have to call me Daddy, darlin'. Not if it makes you uncomfortable, okay? We haven't talked about limits here, and all I wanna do is help you right now. No playing. No scenes. Nothin' like that."

His expression falls, which surprises the hell out of me.

"What's wrong?" I ask, wondering what I might have said to upset him. "I can't make it better if you don't talk to me, honey."

Ryan's tongue darts out to moisten his lips, pink and distracting. "What if…what if I want to play? What if," he clears his throat and meets my gaze, "what if I *need* it?"

Breath catching in my throat, my voice comes out rough when I prod, "What do you need, Ryan?"

"Discipline, Daddy," this time when he says the title, it's with more confidence, but then he hesitantly adds, "please?"

I search his blue-grey eyes for any sign that he's pushing himself past his limits. I wouldn't be surprised if he was: after the experience he had earlier tonight, regaining control would be important to any Sub. But there's nothing in his expression throwing red flags. He's calm, not manic. Any hesitance can be attributed to the newness of the Daddy kink, rather than fear. And that blush –that beautiful, tempting pink flush over his skin— doesn't seem to be caused by shame or anything negative.

It's not difficult to make my decision.

"What kind of discipline, darlin'?"

Relief seems to wash over him. I watch as his shoulders sag and a sheen of tears glosses his eyes before he blinks the moisture away. "Spanking, please. Or a paddle if you have one." He swallows again. "No set count. I…it's not unusual for me to hit subspace with a bit of impact play."

I nod slowly, processing the information. "Thank you for letting me know." Tilting my head, I smile softly, "Do you come when you're spanked?"

I've been with Boys who do and boys who don't, but knowing ahead of time allows me to accommodate the sexual enjoyment into the discipline. For example, if a Boy has been bratty, I might incorporate some orgasm denial as the real punishment.

Ryan bobs his head, his throat working before he answers verbally. "Most of the time, yeah. Usually just before I hit subspace, or as part of it."

"Can you reach subspace without coming?"

"I—" the question seems to stump him for a moment, and he cocks his head in contemplation, his eyes getting a faraway look about them "—don't know. I don't think so."

"That's fine," I assure him, reaching up to cup his jaw, mesmerised by his silver goatee, so neatly trimmed. I stroke his bare cheek with my thumb, feeling the scratch of a day's stubble. "I'm just making sure I do right by you, darlin'." He leans into my touch and closes his eyes, reminding me of an oversized housecat. "Do you have any limits?"

"No degradation or humiliation," Ryan tells me firmly. "And…and I can't kneel or rest on my knees for very long." He hangs his head, adding, "I'm old and it hurts, and not in a fun way."

The embarrassment and sadness in his voice is painful to hear. "Hey now," I try to sound warm and placating while simultaneously wanting to go and put the fear of God into anyone who has shamed him for things out of his control, "you're perfect, Ryan. Besides, people of all ages have physical limitations. It doesn't make playing with you any less enjoyable. In fact," I smirk, "I like gettin' creative."

He lifts his gaze and smiles tentatively back at me, then abuses his poor lip with his teeth again. "What about you? What are your limits?"

"Lying," I answer easily. "You have to be honest with me the whole time. Even if it means pausing to talk things through. If you lie about how you're feeling, I'll know, and I will call red." I try not to think too hard about the man I moved halfway around the world to be with, only to discover his lies. I highly doubt Ryan would be capable of that level of deception…not that whatever is happening between us will go further than tonight, anyway. Clearing my throat, I gently ask, "Will you be honest with me, darlin'?"

Ryan nods. "Yes, Sir." He shakes his head. "Sorry. Yes, Daddy."

He remembered that I don't like to be called 'Sir'.

The effort he's making to accommodate me warms me from the inside, even though I didn't remind him that titles like 'Sir' and 'Master' are a limit for me. I chose not to do so deliberately, because 'Daddy' is so different for him. If we were planning to make whatever this is between us an ongoing thing, I would have said something. But for one night, 'Sir' would have been fine. I just want him to be comfortable.

Nevertheless, I've already told him that if he doesn't want to use the D word, he doesn't have to. I'm not repeating myself. Instead, I smile and lean forward, pressing a soft, chaste kiss to his lips. "Good boy."

He trembles with anticipation, and I pull back from his personal bubble, picking up the t-shirt from the bathroom countertop. Arching an eyebrow at him, I hold it up. "Shirt on or off?"

"Off," he says after only a short moment of consideration.

"Good boy," I reiterate, loving the way the praise makes him shiver. Taking his hand, I lead him back out into the main room, where my gaze swings between the bed, the couch, and the window overlooking the city.

"Would you prefer to be spanked lying down over my lap, or standing up, braced against the window?" I ask him. "Would lying down be better for your joints?"

His chest seems to rise and fall faster as he looks between the bed and the window, once again biting his lower lip. "I love the idea of the window," he admits, "being on show for the city, y'know? But—" he looks back at the bed "— lying down means more connection to you, and if I hit subspace and crash…"

"Bed it is, honey." I cross the short distance from the bathroom door to the king-sized bed, then drop my jeans and tug my shirt over my head, leaving me in my tight, red boxer briefs and nothing else. I wait patiently as Ryan's eyes widen, taking in the ink that litters my skin.

Most were impulse decisions made during my rebellious youth to rattle my conservative parents. Every time my dad would make a comment about me looking more like a 'thug' than a cowboy, I'd reward myself with a new tattoo. The collection of black and grey artwork is eclectic, scattered over my arms, hands, torso, legs, and even on my neck. Cherubs, eagles, Latin text, scorpions, chains, and even a rose can be found illustrated on my skin in permanent, crisp dark ink. There's more on my back, which Ryan gasps at when I turn to pull down the covers, and I wonder whether he feels the same way my pops does.

Ryan's got his own ink, of course. A beautiful, brightly coloured, red Japanese flower set against intricately shaded finger waves in black and grey sits on his right forearm, wrapping around the limb as naturally as you please. But that's it. So it's likely that his piece means something to him, but he's kept the rest of his body free of ink for a reason. Unlike me, treating my flesh like an open canvas, decorating it whenever the whim strikes.

"Your tattoos…" he breathes when I turn around again to face him. His expression isn't critical, though. It's awed. "Wow." He reaches out tentatively to run the pad of his index finger over the thin, intricate lines of the tattoo on my left pec. A weeping angel, hugging her knees to her chest in grief, her long hair obscuring her face, but her wing extended behind her. The gentle touch of his skin on mine feels electric. "These are beautiful."

"Thank you," I acknowledge, not wanting to go into the story behind the myriad tattoos.

Picking up on the message, Ryan pulls his hand back and I immediately miss his touch. But I promised him a spanking, and I always deliver on my promises.

Positioning myself against the headboard, I sit in the middle of the mattress, then gesture for Ryan to join me. "Boxers on or off?" I ask him as he kneels beside my thighs, and he swallows roughly.

"Off."

"Good boy."

He blushes prettily but pushes the cotton down, revealing his hardening cock and a manicured thatch of silvery pubic hair. My mouth waters, but I remind myself yet again that I made this sweet Boy a promise.

"Over my lap," I instruct him, then shuffle sideways until his belly is resting against my left thigh, his hands curled under my right. I place pillows under his knees for a bit more leverage and support, given that he's lying down rather than kneeling. It's not the most usual position for this sort of thing, but it's going to work just fine.

Stroking my hand down the line of his spine, I rest my palm on his bare ass cheek, perfectly rounded and just a bit furry. In another life, and under different circumstances, I would have loved the opportunity to bite into that tempting flesh. Sadly, we only have tonight.

"You comfortable?" I ask him. "Knees okay like this? Not straining your back?"

"I'm good," he says, nodding. He sounds genuinely grateful when he adds, "Thank you, Daddy."

"Good boy," I reward him, watching goosebumps break out over his skin. "Now, what's the safe-word?"

"Red to stop," he tells me dutifully.

"That's right." I wait a beat. "Can you tell me what this discipline is for? You don't have to."

People have many reasons for craving a spanking, many of which include trying to absolve themselves of whatever mistakes they think they've made recently or in times gone by. Others just chase the high of subspace, taken there by giving over control and relishing the pain. And some just find relaxation in giving in to the pain and submission to someone else.

Because I want to know Ryan, even if only for tonight, I want to understand where he's coming from. I want to know whether he fits one of these categories or some mixture of all of them. I want to be able to help him as best I can.

"I…I get antsy," he confesses into the quiet of my hotel room. It's dark, but with the lights from the brightly lit city sprawling outside spilling in from the window, I can see him just fine. He's turned his head to peer up at me while he answers, and the glittering lights from outside the window make his eyes shine. "Regular spankings or paddlings settle me. I don't know why. I get all worked up about…well, life stuff, y'know? All the stupid things I've said or done build up and eat at me, and spanking helps me deal with that."

With the way he seems to subconsciously lean into my touch, I have to wonder how much of his self-administered therapy comes from the spankings and how much comes from the aftercare.

I love the aftercare.

"Thank you for explaining that," I say. Then, after a beat, I ask, "Are you ready to start? Traffic light colour?"

"Yes, Daddy," he answers, and the title seems less stilted now, like he's getting used to saying it. "Green light."

I begin by rubbing the perfect globes of his ass, loving how firm they feel as I warm the skin up beneath my palms. I wait for the tension to melt out of his shoulders before I deliver the first stinging slap to the underside of his left cheek, before swiftly repeating the motion on his right cheek. He flinches on impact but relaxes again until the next swat lands.

I build up momentum, alternating cheeks and landing spots for a few minutes, drawing out the length of time between blows so he isn't quite able to anticipate when I'll strike. When his cheeks start to redden from my slaps, his breathing changes. I make sure to listen for signs of distress, but after landing a firm smack to the middle of his left, fleshy globe, the gasp he releases doesn't sound panicked or fearful. Instead, he sounds mildly pained and a little aroused: just the combination I'm hoping for.

I scale up the force of my next smack, and his body jerks forward, a whimper escaping him as his fingers flex into the underside of my thigh.

"That's it, darlin'," I encourage, keeping my voice low and gentle, "you're taking Daddy's spanking so well."

I bring my hand back down with a resounding *thwack.*

Ryan whimpers again.

"You can get louder," I tell him. "No need to hold back."

I land another couple of smacks in quick succession to what has to be very tender skin by now. His whimpers get a little louder, inching closer to sobs.

"Is this what you need, baby?"

"P-please, Daddy," he moans as I spank him again and again, "more. I…I need…I need to learn a l-lesson…" The words are turning strained, his voice cracking as his tears finally spill over.

I can't help the small frown that tugs my eyebrows together. "What lesson?"

My palm connects with his rosy cheek, and he jolts again. "I was careless," he sobs, and I'm not entirely sure if it's the spanking or the fact that he's thinking about an upsetting topic which has pushed him over the edge, "I m-made stupid decisions—*oh!*"

He cries out as I smack him again.

"Not stupid," I reprimand him firmly, rubbing over the spot I've just made sting. "I don't like that word. Questionable, maybe. But not stupid. You're human, darlin'."

"M-Maddy would have been so disappointed."

I don't know who 'Maddy' is, but the past tense he just used tells me that they're not in the picture anymore. I don't pry. I do, however, deliver another slap to his other butt cheek, making him yelp and squirm. "Other people's opinions aren't important, Ryan. Only yours."

That gets a reaction.

He clenches his eyes shut and his lower lip quivers. I can only see the outline of his profile, highlighted by the light filtering in through the window he's facing, but a pain that I'm sure is more emotional than physical seems to have etched into his handsome features.

Tears roll down his cheeks, some continuing to slide down his neck, others dripping onto the sheets beneath him. He's breathtakingly beautiful and also heartbreakingly sad like this.

"I am disappointed in myself," he whispers, then he turns his face in my direction. His eyes glisten. "Please…please make it go away, Daddy."

Fuck me.

My cock stirs from where it's trapped beneath his chest, and I can do little else than nod and spank him again, and again, and again. He crumbles under my ministrations, letting go of his guilt and anguish, sobbing and babbling as my palm continues to mete out the discipline he begged for.

"That's a good boy," I praise him with genuine warmth. "Let it all out. Then it's done, isn't it? You're taking this so well for Daddy."

His writhing eventually changes pace, and I can tell when subspace begins to creep up on him, his panting turning almost sensual as his sobs switch to mewls and gasps of pleasure.

"Fuck," he breathes, tear-swollen eyes fluttering shut, "Daddy, I'm so hard…"

I don't need to tell him that he's not the only one, because I'm sure he can feel how this is affecting me. Instead, I start to lessen the impact of my swats, knowing that they'll still sting because of how tender his skin is now. "You can come any time, darlin'. I've got you. You've been such a good boy tonight. My good boy."

"S-say it again," he begs me. "C-call me your boy again."

I ignore the squeezing in my chest, wishing that we had met at a different time and place. I'm moving to the other side of the country soon, and I've sworn off long-distance relationships. But for Ryan, I'd be tempted to break that new, self-imposed rule.

"You're my good boy, Ryan." *For tonight, anyway.* "All mine."

"Fuck," he repeats, shifting forward then back, clearly seeking friction against the mattress, "D-daddy…"

I rub his ass again, then land a series of four quick slaps over the heated globes.

That's all it takes. Ryan gasps and shudders, his hips jerking. I feel droplets of his release reach my thigh, and my cock leaks as I think about the intensity of his orgasm. I want to roll him over, to lick up the mess he's no doubt made of his abdomen and the sheets…but I don't.

Instead, I watch his whole body go limp with relaxation. His eyes are half-lidded, glazed and unfocused. A dopey smile lifts one corner of his lips. He's pliant and quiet now, and I decide we're done with the scene.

Gently grazing my hand over his perfectly curved backside, I hiss in sympathy for the heat radiating from his skin. Sitting is going to be painful for a little while, and I hope he's a stomach sleeper for the same reason.

"You did so well, darlin'," I murmur, not wanting to invade the high he's on. I've only had the pleasure of experiencing subspace once myself, during my training as a Dom, but I can recall the floaty, blissful feeling easily enough. It had been complete relaxation to the point of feeling like I'd left my body, almost like my soul was flying. I can understand why some subs become addicted to the sensation, chasing it wherever possible.

Coming down, though? That wasn't pleasant.

Subdrop, for me, was a bitch. Master Brian, the man who trained me, told me it was a double-edged sword: it sucked that I crashed so badly, but it also gave me a better understanding of the importance of aftercare and treating my Subs properly. As if my caregiver tendencies didn't already insist I do just that! Still, I understood his point, and the memories of the crippling depressive episode I felt back then echo in my soul, making me empathise with my Boys when they inevitably come down from subspace.

I let him float for a while, carding my fingers through the soft —now sweaty— hair on his head. My hotel room is high enough from the street that I can't hear any traffic, aside from the occasional faint honk of a horn or blast of a siren. There's no sound in the room apart from our breathing, and it's nice. Peaceful.

The first sign of Ryan coming back to himself is a shuddering sigh, and I stroke his back to ease his transition out of subspace. "Hey, honey," I smile down at him, aware that I need to get him cleaned up, and that his ass needs some lotion. It's a good thing I carry aloe with me at all times. "How are you feelin'?"

"Wrecked," he answers, smiling softly. "But in a good way." He nibbles on his bottom lip. "Thank you for doing this. For everything tonight."

"It was my pleasure, I promise."

His gaze drifts to the bulge in the front of my briefs, to the wet patch where I've leaked so much precum it's almost embarrassing. "But you didn't—"

"I don't need to come to enjoy myself," I assure him softly. "Tonight wasn't about me."

"But—" Pushing himself up and onto one elbow, he reaches for me with his free hand. I catch it with mine and shake my head.

"Not tonight. And, before you go gettin' in your head and jumpin' to self-deprecating conclusions, it's not because I don't want you to. Because I do, Ryan. A hell of a lot."

He frowns, demanding, "Then why?"

"After what you went through tonight, it wouldn't be right, or fair."

Ryan's frown turns into a full-blown scowl. I try not to smile, because it's kind of like being growled at by a puppy; cuter than it is intimidating.

To prevent any further argument, though, I speak before he can get a word in edgewise. "We need to get you and the sheets cleaned up. And I want to rub some aloe on your behind.

You're gonna be feelin' that spanking for a little while, darlin'."

He blushes and wiggles his perfect butt carefully. "That's the way I like it."

I almost say something to the effect of 'good to know', but the words die on my lips before I can verbalise them. It would be good to know if this was going to be more than one night, but it would only hurt us both if I were to pretend this is more than it actually is.

Instead, I gently nudge him from my lap and get him to roll onto his back, with his head on the pillow and his body out of the wet patch that separates us. He winces a little and lifts his hips. "Stay here," I instruct him. "I'll be right back."

It doesn't take me long to grab the bottle of aloe lotion from my bag, or to get a washcloth and get it damp in the bathroom. I snag the spare towel from the counter on my way back into the bedroom, too.

"You don't have to—" Ryan starts to protest when I move to wipe him clean, and I shush him.

"This is part of what I enjoy most about being a Daddy," I explain, gently swiping the cloth over his chest, down his belly, and over his flaccid cock. "Making sure my Boys are properly taken care of." I almost say 'cherished', but that's too much for a one-night thing.

Satisfied that he's clean, I fold the cloth in half and swipe at the wet patch on the bed until I'm satisfied that's clean, too. Then, after wiping off the tiny bits of cum that made it to the side of my thigh, I toss the cloth in the direction of the bathroom and reach for the rolled-up bath towel. I unravel it and then lay it over the wet patch on the sheets.

Happy with that solution, I smile at him and hold up the little bottle of lotion, giving it a shake for good measure. "Roll over onto your tummy, darlin'."

He blushes all over again and bites his lip, but does as I asked. I take a moment to enjoy the effects of my handiwork again, marvelling at the perfect shape of that butt, and the bright red colour my spanking has turned it.

God, he's gorgeous.

I climb onto the mattress on my knees and pop the cap on the lotion, drizzling it into my waiting palm before smoothing it over the warm-to-touch flesh of his ass. He jerks a little at the first touch, but then melts back into the mattress as I gently work the aloe in, knowing that it'll be cooling and soothing the sting from his discipline.

He's practically asleep by the time I'm done.

"Ryan?" I murmur.

"Hmm?"

I can't help finding his groggy response adorable. "Want me to put your shorts back on you?"

"Too sensitive," he mumbles, shaking his head into his pillow. "Come cuddle?"

My heart skips a beat, then squeezes painfully. "Of course, darlin'."

Chapter Five – Ryan

I shrug off my misappropriated jacket before I climb into the driver's seat of my Hilux. After two months living in Denham, I've learned that the jacket is only suitable to wear inside air-conditioned buildings. Honestly, I probably don't need it there, either, but I'm ridiculously attached to it.

The weather here on the northwest coast of Australia is substantially warmer than Brisbane ever was, or at least I'm convinced that it is. And, considering I spend most of my days driving to rural properties, I've learned to dress appropriately for the climate, the job, and the terrain.

Being a country vet is something I'm used to. Once upon a time, Maddy and I ran our own veterinary clinic just outside of Townsville together. Since meeting Maddy, I discovered that I preferred working with livestock to domestic pets, but I lost my passion for it when Maddox died. However, after a year of moping in the city, I itched to get back into my specialised field.

Ha. Field. Get it? Because I work with livestock and on

farms and…yeah, okay, it was a bad pun.

Anyway, when the little clinic in Denham went up for sale, I took it as a sign. Sure, it was on the opposite side of the country to where I lived, but I decided that was what I needed. To start fresh somewhere completely different. There weren't a lot of vets vying for the place, either, so I snapped the business up at a steal, delighted that it came with a lot of loyal, longstanding clients who, let's face it, didn't have many alternative options.

It's been a steep learning curve getting back into the swing of long, rural drives along roads that are little more than gravel tracks and red dirt. Getting used to the smell of farms and remote cattle stations and the dust which seems to settle into my pores, not to mention the heat and the sweat and the long-arse days, has been a *lot*.

A year out of practice made me complacent, and I've spent what little free time I do get trying to work myself back into shape.

But for all that, this whole experience has been healing in a way hiding in Brisbane never was. As much as I miss my friends and family, I feel more myself now after two months in Denham than I did after a year in Brissie.

However, Denham doesn't have much in the way of a nightlife. At least, not the kind I've been itching for.

As my ute rumbles down the dusty road out of town, I glance at my jacket on the passenger seat. Seeing it makes me smile softly to myself, remembering the kind young Dom who gifted it to me. I still feel a little like I stole a treasured possession from him, but when I left his hotel room the morning after my disastrous final night at The Vault, he insisted that I take it with me. I argued that I'd feel more comfortable taking a cheap t-shirt instead, but Oscar just shook his head and pushed the bundle of buttery soft brown leather into my hands.

"It looks better on you than me, darlin,'" he'd said.

I begged to differ, but I kept it anyway. As well as the pair of grey tracksuit pants he gave me to wear, too. I tossed my lamé shorts in the bin and never looked back.

Over the past couple of months, I've thought about Oscar more than what is probably healthy. I've often wondered about his story: why he was in Brisbane, where he was going next, and why such a perfect Dom was out there all alone that night.

I also can't stop thinking about how *right* it felt to call him Daddy.

The way he'd spanked me, taking me to orgasm and then providing the most thoughtful, thorough aftercare…God, he's going to make some Boy very lucky one day.

Jealousy runs through me at the knowledge that it's not going to be me, even if I never considered indulging with Daddy kink before meeting him.

But I'll always have the memories of that night. And I'll always have his jacket. It doesn't smell like him anymore, but every time I put it on, it soothes and warms me from the inside out, like an invisible hug from the man himself.

The ringing of my phone cuts into my thoughts as it blasts through my vehicle's sound system, overriding the radio I keep on for background noise. I press the answer button on my steering wheel and smile, greeting, "Hello, Ryan speaking."

"Doc Sharp?" the voice on the other end of the call asks, sounding a little hesitant.

I glance at the clock on my dash, assuming my receptionist at the clinic has taken her lunch break and diverted calls through to my phone. "The one and the same. How can I help you?"

"Uh, my name's Dusty and I'm callin' from Wombat Run

Station just outside Yalardy." He pauses for a moment before ploughing on, "One of our mares is foaling, but we think the foal is breech."

Immediately, my heart starts hammering. A breech presentation for a horse in foal is one of the most difficult issues to resolve. My brain is already racing through potential complications: damaged internal organs, uterine ruptures, and potentially death to both mare and foal.

"Yalardy, you said?" I start calculating the distance from my current location to the inland town.

"A little west of it, yeah."

At minimum, I'm looking at an hour and a half. Maybe two hours.

"How long has the mare been labouring?"

Dusty answers my questions as I continue driving in his direction, and he also explains that their usual vet, stationed in Yalardy, is currently in the hospital being treated for a snake bite. It's shitty timing all around, really.

"I'm going to keep you on the phone and try and talk you through turning the foal for me, Dusty," I tell him.

He sounds grave when he answers, "Okay."

We both know just how serious this situation is. It's a complicated thing for even a trained equine vet to deal with, but I'm still too far out to risk telling him to wait for me. Even so, the foal's chances aren't looking good; a thought which hurts my heart to think about.

Dusty tells me that he's putting me on speaker, and I can hear him talking to other people as he explains what's happening. Then I start talking him through what he needs to do, asking him questions about what he can feel, and reminding him that he needs to be careful while he reaches inside the mare to try and reposition the foal.

Hope soars inside me when his descriptions sound less like the foal is completely breech and more like its neck and legs are just improperly positioned for delivery.

Asking more questions, tension bleeds from my shoulders when I realise that I'm right. This doesn't mean the foal is out of the woods yet, but its chances of survival just got a whole lot better.

I keep him on the line as I drive, talking him through every step of adjusting the foal's position. By the time I'm about half an hour away, the foal has been delivered successfully. Dusty's relief is palpable when he tells me so, thanking me for talking him through what to do.

"You did the hard part," I tell him, unable to keep from smiling. "I'll be there in about twenty to give mum and baby a check over, though. Go get yourself washed up."

He thanks me effusively, tells me that someone named 'Ozzy' will be waiting for me at the main gate, and then hangs up. Using my hands-free system, I call Sarah, my receptionist-slash-vet nurse, and ask her to reschedule my afternoon appointments to tomorrow, taking a moment to explain what's happened and where I am.

"Bring me a pack of caramel Tim Tams when you get back to town?" she asks playfully. "Y'know, to make up for having to tell Mr. Ziggenfuse that you can't see his baby today?"

Michael Ziggenfuse is extremely precious about his cat. I figure there's a story of some sort there. Nevertheless, I chuckle at Sarah's request. I can only imagine how well that conversation is going to go.

"I'll bring you two packs," I agree. "Thanks, Sez."

"Make sure you get some caffeine in you if you're planning

on making the drive back to town tonight," she says before I can end the call. Even though she's barely twenty-five, Sarah gets very maternal and concerned if she thinks I'm not taking proper care of myself.

I have to admit, it is nice having someone look out for me that way. It fills some of the void since Maddy died.

"I will," I assure her. "I'm sure the guys at the station will be happy to refill my thermos, too."

"Hmm," she replies, not sounding entirely convinced. I can hear her tapping away at her keyboard before she says, "I'm playing with your schedule for tomorrow so you can have a proper lie-in, seeing as you're going to be driving for so long tonight. I don't want to see you in the clinic until nine, do you hear me, Ryan Sharp?"

"Nine?!" I protest. "Sarah—"

"Nine," she cuts me off firmly. "Not a minute earlier. Am I understood?"

Submissive to the core, I back off and make a sound of affirmation at the back of my throat. "Yes, ma'am. Nine a.m. No earlier."

Sarah chuckles before we say our goodbyes and end the call. My GPS leads me to the big, wrought-iron gates of Wombat Run Station ten minutes later, supported on either side by thick brick posts, each one topped with a grey statue of a horse rearing back on its hind legs. Each of the gates also has what I assume is the station's logo —the outline of a wombat bracketed by a drawing of a gumleaf and two gumnuts— set into the iron. The gates are shut, but just as I'm reaching for my phone to call Dusty back, another ute comes rambling down the long, red dirt driveway, kicking up a cloud of red dust on its way to me. It comes to a stop a couple of metres away from the gate.

I roll down my window as the driver climbs out before the dust has even settled, and thanks to the sun being in *just* the wrong spot, all I can see through the glare and the dust is the silhouette of a wide-brimmed hat, broad shoulders tapering down to a trim waist, and thick thighs encased in denim.

God, but I do love living in the country.

"Doctor Sharp, I assume?" the stranger calls jovially as he saunters through the dust cloud he caused.

I don't know if it's my recent musings about my Daddy cowboy, but I swear this guy has a similar American accent. My heart gives a little tug and I almost forget to call back, "Sure am! And you're Ozzy?"

"Yes, sir," he says, voice still raised to account for the distance between him and my ute. "I'll get the gate open; you drive on through and follow the driveway to the main house. I'll close the gate behind us and meet y'all on up there."

That's definitely an American accent...

I squint into the glare of the sun, wishing I could make out more of the guy's features. He sounds young, like my cowboy Daddy was, and I wonder if he's just as attractive. Then I give myself a shake because this level of projecting isn't healthy. "Sounds like a plan."

The gates creak as he unlocks them and wrenches them wide open, and I drive through the gap he's created when he waves me through. I glance through my rear-view mirror in an attempt to catch a better glimpse of him, but then I focus back on the bumpy driveway, following it until a large, sprawling homestead comes into view.

I pull up my ute next to a line of similar vehicles and climb out of the driver's seat, going around to the tray to pull out my medical bag. I'm clipping the tonneau cover back over the edge of the tray when Ozzy parks his ute beside mine. Not long after, his door *clunks* shut, and his boots crunch in the gravel and dirt as he approaches me.

"It's nice to properly meet you, Doctor Shar—*no freakin' way.*" Oscar's pleasant, casual tone shifts to match the shock currently rocketing through my body as I turn to greet him. He's just as handsome as I remember, if a little more tanned from constant exposure to the Western Australian sun. His eyes are wide right now, and the smile on his face is one of awed disbelief. "I can't believe this."

"Neither can I." I blink back at him with my heart in my throat. I'd only been thinking about him a couple of hours ago and now he's literally standing within arms' reach. It's like my daydreaming manifested him or something. I wonder if that works with lotto numbers, too, because these odds seem just as impossible. "Wow."

I have no idea what to do in this situation. Never in my wildest dreams did I think I'd ever again see the man who rescued me when I was at my lowest point. The first man —the *only* man— I've ever called Daddy.

The only man I'd like to continue calling Daddy.

I'm torn between maintaining my professional façade and launching myself at Oscar, wanting to recapture some of the comfort I'd felt when he'd held me in his arms in his hotel room.

But then I have to acknowledge that it has been over two months since that night, and I don't really know all that much about him. He could be in a relationship. He might not do repeats.

He might not be out.

As jagged a pill as that thought is to swallow, I can't help thinking it. After all, he's working on a station in outback Australia: I know I'm stereotyping, but it's a rugged, hyper-masculine sort of environment, and I know from experience that most blokey-blokes out here don't react well to open displays of homosexuality. Admittedly, attitudes have been changing over time, with younger generations much more open and welcoming, but country mindsets seem to take longer to change than those in urban settings.

Oscar's shock seems to fade, and he takes charge of the awkwardness between us, closing the gap in two long strides before he pulls me in for a hug. "It's so good to see you, darlin.'"

Chapter Six — Oscar

Ryan is absolutely the last person I expected to turn up at the station where I'm working now. I mean, I met the guy in a club on the other side of the country, for Christ's sake! But he's here, melting into my hug, and I can't lie and say I'm not elated by this random turn of events.

My mama would probably say it's fate, or God's will, or something airy-fairy like that, but I think it's just the luckiest coincidence in the whole damn world.

I've thought about that night in Brisbane often over the past couple of months. I'm sure I've romanticised it, but the time spent in my hotel room was perfect…and nowhere near long enough. That night, Ryan was the sweetest Boy for me, and even though I've looked into nearby clubs to scratch my itches, I've not yet followed through.

That can't all be blamed on my fixation on the man currently in my embrace, though. I needed a few weeks to properly settle in at the station, to start with. Then, once I was settled, I threw myself into work. The days here are long but rewarding.

Nevertheless, they're exhausting, and by the time I'm flopping into my bunk at night, I'm practically comatose. As such, there haven't been any long drives out to the nearest town for any hanky-panky for me just yet. Hell, I've barely spent time with my right hand!

But now, with Ryan's familiar body pressed against mine, my libido's waking back up. I breathe in his cologne —soft and a touch sweet— and squeeze him for just a moment longer than could be considered appropriate.

"I hear you've been a real good boy," I murmur into his ear, and I delight in the full-body shiver that runs through him. "Dusty said you saved Jemima and her foal over the phone."

I'd been out moving the cattle across from one field to another at the time, but to hear the guys tell it, 'Doc Sharp' had worked a miracle without even being present.

"I didn't do anything," he demurs as he takes a step out of my embrace, putting a professional amount of space between us. I'll let him set boundaries, especially while he's here for work purposes, but I'm not letting him be so dismissive of his own accomplishment.

"You talked him through delivering that foal as if you were right there doin' it yourself. And we both know things might have gone bad if you hadn't."

He falls into step beside me as I start leading the way to the stables. "We were just lucky the baby wasn't breach."

I find it ridiculously cute the way he calls the foal 'the baby'. It says a lot about how much he cares for animals, which isn't really a surprise, considering he's a vet.

"Even so, if you hadn't known exactly what was goin' on and talked Dusty through it the way you did, we'd still be lookin' at the same tragic outcome."

Ryan scoffs and turns to look at me through narrowed eyes, just barely visible through the polarised tint of his sunglasses. Our boots crunch on the gravel as we walk, but I am more focused on him than where we're going. "You're a glass half full kind of guy, aren't you?"

"No sense dwellin' on what could have been, is all I'm sayin'." I shrug. "But seein' as coincidence has delivered you to my feet again, why the hell would I be anythin' other than an optimist?"

His lips twitch behind that sexy as fuck silver goatee of his before he sighs and looks towards our destination again. "It is a pretty great coincidence," he concedes. He waits a beat before nonchalantly asking, "What brought you out here, anyway?"

I've had time to work through the pain and embarrassment of dropping everything to be with a man who lived on the other side of the planet; a process made easier because of the night I spent with the sexy man walking next to me. So, instead of brushing the question off, I answer honestly. "Well, after the man I'd hoped to spend my life with turned out to be a lying, cheating dirtbag, I looked for any sort of farm or ranch — sorry, *station*," I correct myself before Ryan can, "that would have me. Rob was looking for experienced stockmen and stationhands, and I figured moving as far as possible across the country from my ex, if I can even call him that, was a no-brainer."

We're outside the stables now, but Ryan doesn't go in. Instead, his expression morphs into sympathy as he turns to face me properly. "I'm sorry to hear that. But, at the same time, it is good to see you again. I, uh," he rubs the back of his neck, and a pink flush which has nothing to do with the Australian sun climbs up his face, "I've thought about you a lot, actually. Wished that I'd had the balls to ask for your number, if only to thank you properly for what you did for me."

Paying no attention to my colleagues fussing about in the stalls just on the other side of the wide-open doors, I step into Ryan's personal space and tell him, "I've thought about you, too, darlin'. And there ain't no way you're leavin' today without us exchangin' numbers this time."

Instead of balking or getting flustered or shy, like I kind of assumed he might, he grins back at me and, with a hint of sass, says, "Yes, Daddy."

Oh, God, I forgot how fucking hot it is when he calls me that.

While I'm stuck in my pleasantly surprised stupor, he pulls away from our conversation and turns to walk into the stables with a bounce in his step.

Brat, I think fondly, enjoying the view of his perfect ass encased in denim.

"Something you want to share with the class, Ozzy boy?" Jim, one of the other stationhands, asks me with a knowing smirk as he sidles up over from a nearby stall. He's still got a grooming brush in his hand, but Darcy, the dappled mare he was brushing down, seems to be contentedly munching on her chaff and unaware that he's slacking off.

Jim's not much older than me, and he's every stereotype of Australian stockmen come to life. His accent is broad and rural, and I have yet to see him without his black felt Akubra hat. He wears double flapped, two-pocket cotton shirts with long sleeves no matter the weather, and always tan-coloured moleskin pants instead of the jeans the rest of us favour. He's also been my mentor and has become my closest friend since I arrived at the station a couple of months ago.

His gaze follows Ryan as he makes his way to where Dusty and some of the others are still looking after Jemima and her foal like a bunch of first-time dads. "Got a thing for the silver fox vet?"

I shrug, but I'm unable to keep my smile contained. "Maybe. We've met before."

Jim whips his face back in my direction so fast, I'm almost afraid he's hurt himself. "That a euphemism for fucked?"

"Not quite, but," I pause and recall spanking that perfect ass until Ryan came, and my smile gets wider, "close to it."

Jim whistles appreciatively and slugs me in the shoulder. "Well, I'll be damned, Oz."

The best thing about this particular station? The guys are all as rugged and masculine as they come, but they're also the most accepting, open folk I've ever had the good fortune to work with. Not a homophobic or bigoted or racist man among them. Rob must have some kind of hiring-voodoo luck charm or something.

"Yeah," I nod, my attention drawn back to Ryan talking to Dusty outside Jemima's stall. "It was a one-time thing. Never thought I'd see him again. I mean, it happened back in Brisbane."

"Whoa, Brissie? No shit? That's crazy, mate."

"Right?"

"If you believe in signs from the universe, you should probably think of this as one of 'em."

"I'm *way* ahead of you, buddy," I assure him, frowning with disappointment when Ryan disappears out of view, finally entering Jemima's stall. "It definitely feels like somethin'. I'd be stupid to ignore it."

Jim claps his hand on my shoulder and squeezes. "Righto. Well, I'll be gettin' my arse back to Darcy before she thinks I've forgotten her. You go keep an eye on your man."

Have I mentioned how much I love it here?

* * *

Ryan and I exchange numbers after he finishes declaring Jemima and her foal perfectly healthy. We all walk back to the main house to see him off, and Dusty blushes bright red when Ryan casually says he'd make a great vet nurse for how well he followed the directions over the phone.

I've got to admit that watching Ryan in his element is just as hot as seeing him subbing for me. He's confident and intelligent, and he clearly loves animals just as much as I guessed he might.

If I'd thought he was the perfect Boy for me before today, this whole reunion experience is pushing that into dangerous waters, the kind where I start thinking of him as perfect for me in every possible way….and, yes, I know that sounds a little crazy. But, remember: I'm the guy who didn't do his due diligence before packing up my life to be with a man who was *married*. To a woman.

"It's getting late and the boys are all knocking off for the night," Rob says, having also come out to thank the vet who saved his horses' lives, "why don't you join us for dinner before you drive back out to Denham? I'd feel better knowing you've got some food in you before you've gotta make that drive back."

Ryan glances over in my direction with hesitation and I grin back at him, nodding. "We'd love for you to join us. Maybe regale us with stories about your job."

Rob laughs. "That'll make a difference from you lot telling yarns about the cattle." He rolls his eyes as he grins back at Ryan. "They almost had me convinced that the herding dogs were magical."

"They're very intelligent dogs," I insist. "One of the calves got left behind in the back paddock and none of us noticed, but Tilly knew. She hounded us all until we followed her out there."

"Heh," Dusty snorts with amusement, "*hounded*. 'Coz she's a dog."

Ryan laughs heartily at that, and it makes my heart sing.

On the night we met, he was so down and so broken, I had wanted nothing more than to see him smile. Tonight, I'm getting to see him laugh and joke with my new friends and found family, and it's doing things to me that take me right back to those same dangerous waters I mentioned before.

He's gorgeous. With the last rays of the setting sun lighting his skin up in orange tones, he's glowing with beauty, both inside and out. His eyes sparkle with mischief and intelligence, and that smile makes my knees feel rubbery.

"So, what say you, Doc? Joining us for tea?" Jim asks, and I elbow him discretely. He elbows me back.

He raises his left wrist and frowns at his watch before he looks back up and smiles, shrugging before he nods. "Sure. Why not? Beats the two-minute noodles I'd make once I got back home, I'm sure."

I immediately want to scold him for not eating right, but I manage to contain those urges for the time being. The next time I get him alone —and there *will* be a next time— I'll make sure he's taking care of himself. But for now, I laugh with the others, narrowing my eyes as Rob claps him on the shoulder again, and then follow everyone up to the main house to wash up for dinner.

Chapter Seven – Ryan

It's not a surprise to find myself seated beside Oscar at the dinner table. (I say 'table', but it's actually three long timber dining tables set together to make one super long one, taking up what was probably intended to be both the formal living room and dining rooms.) The chairs are an eclectic mix of styles, and the whole look really sets off the country vibe of the station's main house.

It's warm and inviting in here, the cream-painted walls decorated with photos in a variety of different sized and shaped frames. They're displaying everything from the animals, to the staff, to the family who owns the place.

The stationhands are all seated along the dining table, chatting animatedly and passing bowls and trays of steaming dishes whose combined scents are making my mouth water and my stomach grumble.

It's been a long time since I had a proper homemade meal. I usually buy pre-made stuff from Woolies. There's no sense making a fuss just to feed myself, and Maddy was always the better cook of the two of us anyway.

A mild pang of grief strikes me as I think of Maddy. He would have loved it here. Being a country vet had been in his blood: he was the one who had gotten me into it, after all. He'd loved rural Australia and everything that comes with it, right down to the constant flies and the snakes.

I suppress a shudder. I don't like snakes. Thankfully, I haven't had to treat many during my career…and, yes, I'm aware there's an irony in being a vet with a fear of a specific kind of animal. So sue me, I didn't grow up in the country; I was always a city boy before I met Maddox.

I'm shaken from my thoughts as an arm reaches across in front of me and lifts my plate from its setting. Oscar sets about piling on steaming heaps of meat and veggies before he places it back down in front of me, his eyebrow raised expectantly.

I try to suppress the full-body shiver that expression induces.

"Thank you," I say, managing to bite off the instinctive 'Daddy' before I can embarrass myself among his colleagues. The way Oscar's lips twitch suggests that he heard it loud and clear anyway.

Heat rises to my cheeks. I don't understand why I have those urges now. Sure, the night with him had been mind blowing and perspective changing, but I'm so much older than him. Submitting to him as a Dom is one thing, but thinking of him as Daddy? Isn't that…weird?

How is it any weirder than wanting to call him Sir? I question myself. *Or Master?*

Titles he's uncomfortable with.

Maybe *that's* why I want to call him Daddy, because I know he doesn't like the alternatives. I've Googled a lot since that night in Brissie, and I've been reassured that Daddy kink doesn't have to include regression play. It's not that I think there's anything wrong with age regression, mind you, but it just doesn't appeal to me.

I want to submit…but I kind of like the idea of being taken care of, too.

Maddy used to do both for me.

I have to close my eyes and take a deep breath. Maddy's been gone for almost a year and a half. I can't be thinking about him while I think about a new man, can I?

Even while I try, my brain won't let go of my previous train of thought.

Maddy was more than just my Dom. I called him Sir when we played, but he took care of me as well as dominating me. I always put that down to him being my husband, but…I never took care of him in quite the same way. He made sure that I ate right. He dealt with all the confusing paperwork to do with our business. He generally made all the big, scary decisions for me, and I trusted him to take that stress off my shoulders.

After a couple of months of Googling, I'm coming to realise that I might have called him Sir and thought of him as my Dom, but he was actually more of a Daddy Dom.

Huh.

Maybe I'm interested in Oscar being my Daddy because I miss having one. Even if I never used the word before, that *was* my dynamic with Maddy. And, if I push the logic a little further, maybe that's why interacting with other Doms felt inherently wrong after Maddy died. Yeah, I was grieving him, but I was also looking for the wrong kind of Dom, too.

"You okay, darlin'?" Oscar's breath ghosts over my neck as he leans in to ask me the question, his voice low and calming.

Yeah, I consider replying, feeling lightheaded, *just having a lightbulb moment.*

Clearing my throat, I nod. "I'm good," I assure him, smiling to let him know that I appreciate his concern. "I was just…lost in thought."

"Well, you should eat up before Jim pounces on your plate," he replies, jutting his chin to gesture to my other side.

The man in question —Jim— grins unrepentantly back at me when I turn to face him, his previously full plate already half-empty. "It's the quick or the dead here, Doc. Gotta sink your teeth in before someone snatches your tasty treat away."

I blink in surprise while Oscar groans.

"Ignore Jim," he says, and I glance back to catch him shooting a pointed glare at his colleague, "he's got no hope of sinkin' his teeth into anythin' you might want."

"You guys aren't talking about the roast, are you?" Dusty asks from across the table. His eyes dart from Jim, to me, to Oscar and then back again. His cheeks turn pink when Jim laughs heartily.

"I'm just fucking with them, Dust," Jim says, waving his hand dismissively as he leans back in his seat. He tilts his head back in a stretch, and he misses the flash of relief across Dusty's youthful face. But I don't.

My mind is spinning.

My shock must be written all over me, and Oscar interprets it correctly because he snorts and says, "Don't mind us, Rye. I think you'll find this is the most progressive, accepting station in the whole damn country. I got pretty lucky landin' here with these degenerates." His thigh, warm and firm, nudges mine beneath the table. "Now, eat up like a good boy, hmm?"

Fuck, but that endearment goes straight to my cock.

I shift in my seat and lift my knife and fork, finally digging into my dinner. It's just as delicious as it smells. Once he's seemingly satisfied that I'm eating, Oscar resumes his meal, too.

When I'm certain I can't fit another morsel in my mouth, I lean back in my chair and rub my belly. I'm full and content… and sleepy.

That's not good.

It's a three-hour drive back to Denham and driving our country roads at night is bad enough when you've got your wits about you. Being sleepy is basically begging for trouble.

"You okay there, Doc?" Jim asks, and it takes far too much effort to turn my head to face him. He's still eating, mopping up a puddle of gravy with a home-baked bread roll. He furrows his eyebrows in concern. "You look dead tired, mate."

"Mmm," I agree, patting my belly. "I think I ate too much. Should probably have some coffee before I hit the road."

Jim glances over me momentarily before he meets my gaze and shakes his head. He's still holding his sopping roll over his plate. "Yeah, nah. You're not driving in this state. You'll probably run off the road or something. I reckon you should crash here for the night and head out early. We'll likely be up before you anyway."

"Oh, no, I couldn't put you all out any more than I already have."

My protest seems to land on deaf ears, because Jim whistles shrilly to catch his employer's attention. "Oi, Rob. Can Doc Sharp crash in one of the guest houses tonight? He's buggered and I don't think he'd be safe on the roads like this."

My cheeks burn as every set of eyes around the table lands on me. "I'm fine," I insist, but they all shake their heads.

"'Course you're welcome to stay the night," Rob declares

cheerfully. "Being midweek, most of the guest houses are empty right now. We operate a side-hustle as a farmstay, y'see. Get a lot of city slickers out here on weekends and school holidays." His grin turns affectionate. "It's good to see the kids getting into all the farm stuff. They like feeding the animals, collecting eggs…better than seeing them all glued to screens. Gives me hope that some'll keep the stations going when we're all gone, y'know?"

"Dear God, who gave him the Bundy? He's off on his 'we'll all be dust' rant again." Another guy jokes from the other end of the table, holding up his half-empty glass, giving it a little shake. "Also, can I have some?"

"Get your own," Rob sasses back at him, reaching for the bottle in question. "It's a work night anyway."

The guy snorts. "You my Boss or my Daddy, Rob?"

"Either way, I'll tan your hide if you drink my rum."

"Jesus," I exhale in surprise and sit back in my seat again, shaking my head. "You lot really are a different breed, aren't you?"

Oscar laughs and rubs my back, which wakes me up more than a cup of coffee possibly could have. "I told you," he all but croons into my ear, his honeyed accent doing all sorts of things to my nerve-endings, "it's the most progressive, accepting, half-queer bunch of ranchers I ever worked with."

"Stationhands," Jim huffs. "We don't do ranches here."

"Whatever," Oscar dismisses him lazily. "It's all the same thing."

Instead of taking the bait, Jim leans forward and winks at me. "Want me to show you to your room for the night, Doc?"

"Hell no," Oscar answers for me, and he snakes a possessive arm around my shoulders to match his tone. "I'll be showin' the nice doctor to his room."

"Uh-huh. His room or yours?"

"Well," Dusty cuts in, his eyes darting between all three of us much like they had earlier, his brow furrowed and chapped pink lips pinched with displeasure, "seeing as Ozzy's bunking with me, I think he'd be better off showing Doc to his own room."

In this moment, Dusty reminds me of a little terrier. He's short in stature, but he's territorial and yappy. I like him a lot. I can't help grinning at him. "Or maybe you can show me where I'm staying?"

"Now, hang on, darlin'…" Oscar starts, and I don't have to look at him to know that he's frowning. "I'm more than capable of gettin' you home safe for the night."

Jim says something teasing in response, but my mind has already flashed back to that night at The Vault. "I know," I reply softly, knowing that he gets my meaning as soon as the words are out.

His arm tenses around my shoulder, and he leans into my personal space again. I brace myself for whatever sweet, charming thing he's about to say, when the moment is interrupted.

"Oz, the keys for cabin three are on the hook in the kitchen," Rob's voice cuts in from down the table. "Figure Doc Sharp might enjoy a room with a view." I look down the length of the table and the station owner grins at me. "Consider it thanks for saving Jemima and Little Ted."

A laugh escapes me before I can stop it. "You named the foal Little Ted? And its mother is Jemima?" Narrowing my gaze, I lean forward a little. "Do you have a chicken named Henny Penny and a cow named Daisy? A cat named Diddle, even?"

Rob's lips twitch, but Dusty's awed "How'd you know that?"

is what sets off my guffaws.

Dusty, who is probably only in his early twenties, should probably remember Play School better than I do. I'm not ashamed to admit that a lot of my memories come from watching it while high or drunk during my uni days.

Don't judge me: I was at uni before we had such things as wifi or streaming services. And when you're high or drunk as fuck, nothing is more amusing than Spike Milligan's *On The Ning Nang Nong* sung by underpaid NIDA graduates on low-budget community television.

But I digress.

Still chuckling, I shake my head. It's not every day you meet a bloke's bloke like Rob only to discover that he has a weakness for classic Australian preschool entertainment. "Your animals are all named after Play School toys," I inform Dusty, only for him to appear more confused.

"Play School?" he asks. "Like…preschool?"

"The TV show," Jim tells him. "It's been on the ABC since the seventies or something." He smirks, and, as an aside, adds, "I had a crush on Noni Hazelhurst as a kid."

"I always said you had good taste," Rob snarks.

"None of these words are making any sense," Dusty's complaint makes me feel old.

"To you and me both," Oscar agrees, but he sounds amused. "I feel like Google will be our friend later."

"Or right now." Dusty whips his phone from his pocket and taps at the screen. He screws up his face as he stares at his screen, and the very song I recalled only moments ago starts playing through the tinny speaker.

"That's what passes for kids TV in this country?" Oscar asks, sounding horrified. "I didn't think things were that dire here. I mean, cartoons have been a thing for a long while. Disney…Hanna Barbera…" The look he casts me is full of exaggerated concern and he gestures at Dusty's phone. "You didn't have to live this way, darlin'."

Down the table, Rob bursts into guffaws. "You wash that mouth of yours out with soap, Ozzy. Play School's iconic. It raised generations of kids."

"My own included," I nod in agreement, then blink as the table around me falls silent.

"You've got kids?" Oscar asks gently. His tone is unreadable.

I feel myself flush. "Maddy —Maddox, my…my late husband— did. They were already almost in their teens by the time Maddy and I got together, but I think of them as my own, yeah."

Even now, they both check in with me every couple of weeks to make sure I'm taking care of myself. Neither of them were happy with me when I told them I was moving across the country, but they understood that I needed to start fresh again.

Thinking fondly of them, I continue to talk into the surprised silence. "Makayla, *Mak*, is thirty now, and Trev's twenty-eight." It's at this moment I realise just how close they are in age to Oscar. "They're great kids. She's a paediatrician in Toowoomba, and he's a lawyer in Brissie. Criminal law."

As I talk, I can't help but wonder…will they be disgusted if Oscar and I become a thing? And, God, will he think it's weird that I've got step kids his age?

A dim stirring of memory settles my nerves a little. I *did* originally tell him that I was old enough to be his dad, and he was okay with that.

More than okay, my brain says helpfully. *He's into older men.*

But then maybe I'm getting ahead of myself. Yeah, he's shown interest in me today, but that doesn't mean he wants anything between us to become serious or ongoing. He might just want to let off a little steam. God knows he earned it the night he rescued me. I was the one who got off back then, not him.

"You sound so proud of 'em," Oscar says softly. I turn my head to find him smiling. "I bet they're great people. They sure sound smart, at least. But then, you're a vet, so…" he trails off, shrugging.

"Maddy was, too. He was an equine specialist, actually." I grin at Dusty. "That's how I knew so much about how to help Jemima without seeing her. Maddy was obsessed with horses. Some of that rubbed off on me."

After over a year grieving him, it feels liberating to be able to talk about my late husband without crying. To feel the fond exasperation thrumming through my veins when I think about just how horse-crazy he was. Not that I was any different after I started working with him.

"Is that why you're a country vet?" Oscar asks, pulling my attention back in his direction. He's got his head cocked to the side and genuine curiosity in his eyes.

I tilt my own head from side to side. "Eh…kind of? I tried my hand at returning to suburban practice back in Brissie, but I missed the rural life. Maddy and I had our own practice just outside of Townsville. His enthusiasm for working with horses was infectious, y'know? I'd been content with cats and dogs until I met him. Then, suddenly, I was almost as obsessed with livestock as he was. After he died, I sold the practice and moved to Brisbane…" I trail off with a shrug. "A year of that was enough for me to realise that I really missed working out in the country. When the practice in Denham went up for sale, it felt like I'd be getting the best of both worlds. I see a lot of domestic pets as well as livestock nowadays."

Somewhere in the middle of my rambled answer, Oscar placed his hand on my back. Now, he rubs soothingly, then squeezes my shoulder. "I'm so sorry for your loss, darlin'. You sound happy when you talk about him. About Maddy."

"I was happy. *We* were happy." I smile back at him, grateful that he doesn't seem irritated or put-out to hear me talk about my dead husband.

"How'd he die?" Dusty asks, and Jim groans.

"Mate, you can't just ask that."

"Why?" Dusty pouts, then sits back and stretches his arms out at his sides, gesturing to the table at large. "We were all thinking it."

Sure enough, everyone seems to be following my tale of woe with rapt attention. Don't they get streaming services out this way? Surely my depressing story isn't that entertaining.

Jim just sighs and says, "Because you just *can't*, Dust. It's rude."

"It's okay," I cut back in as Dusty's expression falls. He's a sweet kid, and I like being able to talk about Maddy without the oppressive veil of sympathy or sadness which usually accompanies talking to family or old friends. "I don't mind." My smile still slips as I answer, "It was skin cancer. Melanoma. It spread fast and—" I stop abruptly as my eyes fill with tears and my voice breaks, remembering just how quickly my vibrant, sixty-three-year-old husband's health plummeted. Oscar squeezes my shoulder, his hand a steadying warmth. Clearing my throat, I finish, "He was gone pretty suddenly."

Dusty stares back at me, horrified. "I'm so sorry. I shouldn't have asked. I…shit, Doc, I'm sorry."

A watery chuckle escapes me and I shake my head. "Don't

be." Cringing, I add, "I'm sorry for bringing the mood down. How'd we get from Play School to this?"

"Let's just blame Dusty," Jim teases, and I snort at the affronted expression on the younger man's face.

Oscar lets go of my shoulder to pat me on the back. It's as much a calming gesture as it is a giddy-up. "C'mon, darlin', I think that's our cue to get you set up in your guest quarters."

The words remind me of how tired I am, and I nod. "Okay. Thanks."

Pushing to my feet, I thank Rob again for his hospitality, compliment the food one last time, then bid the rest of the team goodnight and, for the most part, goodbye. I can't imagine they'll be needing me to travel out from Denham again, not once their local vet is back on his feet.

It's a bit sad to realise, really. This station is unlike any other I've visited, and I could see myself befriending this whole group if I was given enough time to do so.

Then, with Oscar's palm warming the middle of my lower back, I wonder if maybe I might get that chance one day after all.

It's probably wishful thinking, but I could use some wish magic right now.

Chapter Eight — Oscar

That was a lot, I think to myself as I lead Ryan back to our parked cars after swinging past the cupboard in the foyer to grab the keys for his cabin for the night. *Poor Ryan.*

From our first —though limited— meeting, I knew that he had some kind of history, but learning that he's recently widowed makes my heart ache for him. Knowing about it doesn't change my attraction to him, nor does it change my desire to pursue a relationship if he also wants one, but it does make me feel even more protective of him. It also reminds me that I need to be patient with him, because not only is he inexperienced with my brand of kink, he's also grieving.

I might not have lost a partner, but I know that the death of a loved one isn't something you just get over like you would a breakup. Maddy was Ryan's husband, someone he loved until the guy took his last breath. Someone he still loves and probably always will. Someone whose memory I have no intention of replacing. Nor do I have any intention of taking

Maddy's place in Ryan's life or his heart.

But I still want a place of my own there, too, one day.

Could I share Ryan with the memory of his husband? Is he ready for me to try? Is it something he even wants right now? Or ever?

Obviously, I have to talk to him about it. I think about what I'll say and how I'll say it during the short drive out to the guest cabin, checking in my mirror that Ryan is following me. Call me an overprotective Daddy if you have to, but with the daylight having dwindled away, the dirt drive can be a bit bumpy and daunting to those new to the property. I'd hate for him to hit a pothole, or for him to end up travelling off course.

When I get to the little timber cottage, I head to the front door and unlock it, flipping on the lights just as Ryan parks his truck beside mine. He climbs out of the cab of his truck and slings a dark-coloured duffel bag over his shoulder.

I raise an eyebrow at that.

"I always travel with a change of clothes," he explains, catching my expression and interpreting it correctly. "Never know what can happen when you're working with animals."

"That's real smart of you," I tell him. "Good boy."

In the yellow light from the cottage's single oyster-shaped ceiling light, he blushes. "It's just logical. After my third experience getting dirt and blood all over me, I decided I always needed a backup plan. People don't like it when their vet turns up looking like he went full American Psycho on his last client."

My laugh bursts out of me before I can stop it. "Yeah, I'd probably think twice about lettin' someone covered in blood look after my dog if I had one."

He grins and then gets distracted looking around the cottage. It's all one open-plan space, with timber walls painted white, polished timber floors, a queen-sized bed, a potbelly stove fireplace, a little kitchenette and a tiny table with two golden-hued timber chairs. On the far side of the room from the front door, there's another door which leads to the bathroom: a cozy space with a shower over a claw-footed tub, a vanity and a toilet.

"This is really sweet," Ryan says, smiling softly as he takes it all in. "I can understand why Rob is booked out on weekends and holidays."

Most of the guest cabins here have the same layout, but some are a little bigger and have an additional bedroom to accommodate for families. There's also the honeymoon cabin, too. That one is just like this one, only it has a larger fireplace and a corner spa tub. All-in-all, there are eight guest cottages on site, and Rob has plans to build more over time.

I nod. "It's a working station, but when you drive out tomorrow —follow the gravel road back down to the main house, then from there head on down to the gate— you'll head past what we call the petting zoo: the pens where the pigs are kept, the sheep paddock, and the chicken coop. People really love the sheep for some reason."

"There's a lot going on here," he muses. "No wonder Rob's got so many staff."

"He gets extra hands in at peak times, too. He's a fair boss, and he's got a good schedule goin' for runnin' the place. I really lucked out gettin' a job here."

Ryan's gaze shifts from taking the room in and settles back on me. He cocks his head and, after a moment where I guess he was deliberating whether to ask or not, he says, "Well, you know the bones of my sob story. Did you want to tell me yours? You said something about a lying, cheating ex?"

I cringe, feeling like what I went through pales in comparison to his trauma. When I tell him as much, he huffs and sits on the edge of the bed, patting the space beside him. I sit, because I enjoy his presence too much to turn him down. He smiles softly. "You know that trauma isn't a competition. Your feelings and pain aren't less valid than mine just because there wasn't any death involved. Heartache is heartache, no matter the catalyst for it."

Well, I can't argue with that, can I?

"I'd ask how you got so wise, but knowing even a little of what you've been through makes the question kind of dumb." I lean in and bump his shoulder with mine playfully to lighten the mood. "And you're right. I just feel like admitting just how stupid and trusting I was might shake your trust in me as a Daddy. Assuming you were even interested in—"

"I am," he interrupts me quickly. "Interested in you, I mean. In exploring that whole Daddy Dom/Boy dynamic further." His skin turns pink again and he rubs his palm over his face. "God, I hope that's where you were going with it. Not that I'd say no to a one-night thing, either, but…I'd like more if you do, too."

Oh, this sweet, sweet Boy.

"Honey," I croon, shaking my head as he tries to look away, "I want more than one night with you, too." I'd like *all* the nights, but I keep that tidbit to myself. I don't think either of us wants to feel like a relationship between us is a rebound. Instead, I finish with, "I know we don't really know each other, but I'd like that to change. And I think, judgin' by that night in Brisbane, there's potential for somethin' special between us."

He's quiet for a moment and I wait patiently, letting the sounds from outside —the cicadas, crickets and the occasional bleat of an animal in the distance— fill the short void. Eventually, Ryan ducks his chin and confesses, "I think so, too."

I want to whoop with joy, but I settle for an easy grin. "Then that's settled. When can I take you on a date, sweet boy?"

I want so badly to be able to officially say that we're dating.

Ryan laughs and flops back onto the mattress, rolling onto his side and propping himself on his elbow as he smirks up at me. "You move fast, huh?" Before I can defend my honour, he adds, "And, anyway, don't think you're getting out of telling me your tragic backstory." The playful twinkle in his eye fades, and he reaches towards me with his free hand. Squeezing my thigh gently, he says, "I'm not going to think less of you."

Snorting, I refute, "You haven't heard what a fool I was yet."

"It sounds like you trusted someone you loved. There's nothing foolish about that."

"You're smooth, you know that?"

"Oscar," his tone is serious. "When we met, you told me your limits were honesty above all else. That needs to go both ways. I'll tell you everything and anything about Maddy and my marriage that you want or need to know, but I expect the same courtesy in return if we're going to make anything between us work."

"You're right, darlin'." I sigh. "I know you are. But...I was a real idiot, y'know? Any heartache I went through is my own damn fault. And, more than that, I'm embarrassed by it all. I'm a Daddy. I'm supposed to have my head on straight. I mean," letting out a bitter laugh, my shoulders slump, "how can I ask a Boy to trust me to make decisions for him if my own track record is shot to hell?"

There's another pause where Ryan considers me for a long moment, then he pushes himself back up and off the mattress and points towards the headboard. "Lie down," he demands, and it's such a surprise to be bossed around by someone I know to be incredibly submissive that I comply.

After crawling into place on the left side of the bed —my usual side— I watch as he follows and takes the right side. Then he opens his arms and I roll willingly into his embrace until he's spooned against my back.

I'm not used to being the little spoon.

This is…nice. Strange, but nice.

"Now," he says, and his generally soft voice rumbles through his chest at my back, "is it easier for you to talk about it if you're not looking at me? Because I met you *after* whatever hurt you happened, and you were everything I needed that night. You were the perfect Daddy Dom, and I trusted you then and I'll keep on trusting you after tonight."

"But—"

"You know how I'm so sure?" The question is rhetorical because he answers it without my input. "I'm sure because you wouldn't be so worried about being a good Daddy if you weren't already a good Daddy."

Should I have expected anything other than logic from my new Boy? I mean, the man is a vet, for Christ's sake. He's smart as hell, and I love it. When we really get going, I'm sure he's going to keep me on my toes.

"Alright," I concede, grinning as his hold around my waist tightens a little. But, honestly, where do I start? "So, I've been a Daddy Dom for a while now. Ten years or so. I trained at a club in New Orleans and when I say I've seen everythin', darlin', I saw most of it there in those early days."

"Sounds like it would have been a great eye-opener."

"For a kid like me from a tiny little churchgoin' town in

Texas, you bet your sweet ass it was." I chuckle. "Of course, the internet opened my eyes long before I went out lookin' to explore my kinks. But that's a whole other story."

He hums. "I am a little jealous that I missed out and had to have my whole sexual and kink awakening the old-school way: sneaking naughty magazines and hiding them under a mattress…or, after I turned eighteen, being shit scared of getting caught going to the adult stores on gay porn and kink nights in their little cinemas."

"I have *so* many questions," I tease, imagining him as a skittish teenager blushing through his sexual awakening. "But I'll keep 'em to myself for now."

"Good, because I believe you were telling me a story."

"So I was." I snuggle further into his embrace. The warmth of him at my back and wrapped around me is something I can definitely get used to. "Right. So, I knew early on I wanted to be a Daddy Dom, but it wasn't until midway through my training —when I was practicing a sensory play scene with a gorgeous silver fox of a sub— that I realized I had a real thing for older men."

He squeezes me again and nuzzles that gorgeous goatee of his against the back of my neck. "I hadn't noticed," he murmurs playfully as my body reacts and I shiver.

"You're not playing fair, sweet boy. I might need to call you my naughty boy, instead."

"Only if you'll spank me, too, Daddy. Otherwise, that's just mean."

I groan, telling my cock not to get any ideas. "Did you want me to keep telling the story or not?"

"Sorry, Daddy." His apology does nothing to curb my libido. "Continue."

After clearing my throat, I say, "I've had a few long-term Daddy/Boy relationships over the years. Two of the three of them were with older men. All ended amicably. I kind of prided myself on that."

"Honesty and communication."

"Exactly." I smile, but it fades as I reach the point of my wind up. "Anyway, as you can imagine, being gay in the South has its challenges. Add my personal kinks and then my preference for older men to that and I found myself getting lonely after I went back to my parents' ranch in Texas to help 'em through some tough times…not that my pops or mama were particularly appreciative. We love each other, but it works better at a distance, y'know?"

"Mmmhhmm. So you were lonely. I can relate to that."

My sweet Boy.

"I'm hoping we'll help each other not feel that way anymore."

"Me too. Now. Story."

"Don't be bossy, honey. That's my job."

At my back, he huffs and I feel his breath ghost over my skin and ruffle my hair.

"Anyway," I force myself back on topic, fighting the urge to roll in his arms and kiss him senseless. "I was lonely, and I went online and joined a whole heap of Discord chats and Facebook groups and dating apps lookin' to connect with someone. Then I met Richard online and he ticked all my boxes." Ryan's arms tighten around me again, because it's obvious where this is going. "We chatted for months, then Facetimed. I fell head over heels for his accent and his personality and…well, just *him.* He lived in Brisbane and spun tales about the future we'd have together, and I believed him. So, after my parents and I had another fight about me doin' everythin' in my power to not fit in, I decided it was time to follow my dreams for good. I sold my truck and just about everythin' I owned, got myself a passport, organised my VISA and right to work stuff, got myself a ticket to Brisbane, and I flew my smalltown-USA ass out to Australia to surprise my Boy."

"Oh no."

Snorting bitterly, I nod. "Oh yes. So, I'm jetlagged and buzzing on pure adrenaline when I get to his house —because he'd given me his address when we started sendin' each other gifts— and I don't know which one of us was more horrified when we finally met. Me, him, or his wife and kids."

Shame and embarrassment wash over me as I relive the moment where time had stopped. Guilt, too, because I'm pretty sure my unannounced arrival destroyed his marriage…though I'm not so messed up that I can't see that it's all his own fault for cheating to begin with.

But he wasn't cheating *on* me. He was cheating *with* me. And even if I didn't know it, I feel complicit. Dirty. Not good enough for the sweet man holding me against his chest and murmuring condolences in my ear, that's for sure.

"Jesus," Ryan breathes, squeezing me tightly, "I can't imagine what you were feeling. Like having the rug pulled out from under your feet, but even worse because it was by someone you trusted." His tone turns indignant. "What a wanker," he huffs out. "I'm so sorry you went through that."

"It was my own fault. I'm the idiot who made the snap decision to surprise his online boyfriend…"

"You're not an idiot. How were you supposed to know he was lying to you? That he was married? Did he ever tell you?"

"Of course not!" I don't mean to sound quite so defensive as I jump to refute the idea. Taking a breath, I apologise. "Sorry.

It's just…I'd never be that person."

"I know," Ryan's tone is still soft and understanding. "Honesty and open communication. That's your thing, Daddy."

For all that I've been blaming myself for the mess with Richard, hearing the conviction in Ryan's voice has my throat tightening as relief sets in.

He doesn't think I'm an idiot.

"It's pretty fitting his name was Richard," he continues to muse as I try to get my emotions back under control. "Dick is a very appropriate nickname for him. The dick." He spits the last two words with venom and snuggles up against me. "I hope karma gets him."

"You believe in karma?" I find that strange. He's a man of science and medicine, for one thing. For another, what kind of terrible things does he think he and Maddy did to deserve the hand they were dealt in life?

I feel him shrug. "I like the sentiment, but I don't actually believe there's a universal power that dishes out consequences to dicks like him or anything."

"I'll admit, I wouldn't hate it if a piano fell on him or somethin'."

Ryan chuckles. "Well, we can just imagine it, hmm?"

This is the moment I give in to the urge to roll over to face him, warmth suffusing me at the playful smile pulling at his lips. I swear his eyes are glinting with it, too.

With his arms still wrapped around me, I feel cared for. Wanted, and not just sexually…though there is a definite bulge brushing against mine, which suggests that he's just as affected by our proximity as I am. It's been a long time since I haven't felt lonely, and I want to revel in how nice it is just to be held.

But I've *just* told the story of how I ended up living so far from home, and it feels like maybe I need to learn from that whole experience.

Don't go throwin' all your eggs in one basket so quickly again, says the little voice in my head which still sounds irritatingly like my mama.

Then Ryan's expression turns almost shy as he quietly says, "Hi," and that voice vanishes from my thoughts.

"Hi," I smile back at him, my insides buzzing at the way he nibbles at his lip.

"Is this okay?" he eventually asks. "Holding you like this?"

"Darlin', I—" I almost say 'could die a happy man right now' and only just manage to catch myself. *Don't make jokes about death to the widower.* "I really like it," I say instead. "Truth be told, it's been an age since anyone last held me like this. It's nice. Especially with you."

Oh, that gorgeous blush of his...

With pink cheeks, he admits, "It's been a long time for me, too. I've missed this."

"Were you the big spoon with Maddy? Wait, shit, sorry. I probably shouldn't be mentioning him while we're gettin' all cosy, should I?"

The startled look in his eyes softens and he shakes his head. "I don't mind. It doesn't make me feel weird or sad or anything." He leans back a little and frowns. "Unless it's weird and uncomfortable for you."

"Nah," I brush his concern off, "I'm the one who brought him up."

"You sure? I can't imagine hearing me talk about my ex is all that appealing for you."

I'm already shaking my head before he's finished talking. "One, he's not *just* an ex. And I'm adult enough to know that

I'm not gonna be competing with a dead man. I want you to tell me about him, if you're comfortable with it. Everythin' and anythin' you want to tell me."

Ryan smiles and nods. "I've met men twice your age who aren't anywhere near as mature as you."

"Yeah, well, I'm a Daddy. It wouldn't work so well if I wasn't."

"Mmm," he agrees, thoughtfully. "But you're a Daddy who likes being the little spoon?"

"Actually...you're the first Boy to hold me that way. I'm usually the big spoon. But...I did like it. With you."

His lips pull into a self-satisfied smile. "Yeah, well, Maddy was usually the big spoon, too. Turns out, I like it both ways." He waggles his eyebrows and my cock twitches in interest.

"Oh, is that so?" I smirk. "I'm all for it if my Boy wants to top every once in a while."

"Fuck," he rasps and seems to instinctively buck his hips forward, once again rocking our clothed cocks against each other. "It's been a long time since I...well, it's been a long time in general, really. But...I could be a born again top."

Smiling at his playful side, I still insist, "Honey, we'll go at your pace. You tell me what you want, and if I can make it happen, I will."

"Can I blow you, Daddy?"

If I don't come in my pants at just the question...

I swallow roughly and nod. My voice is strained as I answer, "I'd love that, darlin'."

He reaches for my belt buckle, then hesitates. "Or," he starts to suggest, his blush slowly deepening in the most adorable way, "Maybe we could...uh...sixty-nine?"

He's so damn sweet, it's going to kill me.

"God, yes!" I tug him in by his belt loops, kissing his lips soundly while I get his jeans unbuckled and unzipped. "You're a smart one, aren't you, sweetheart?"

He moans and nuzzles his cheek against mine when I palm his hard length through the soft cotton of his underwear.

"Daddy," he exhales, sounding needy and desperate, "more. Please."

"More what?"

"Everything."

Chapter Nine – Ryan

It takes no time at all to undress each other, which is both fantastic and disappointing. It's been a long time since I've undressed another man, or had one undress me, and I both want to savour the experience and also get to the naked part.

I am *not* disappointed when we're both stripped bare and Oscar's inked body is on display. I've seen his exposed chest and legs before, but taking in the smooth, youthful skin, inked like a fine canvas, takes my breath away all over again the second time.

"I love your tattoos," I tell him, reaching out to run my fingers over the angel on his left pec. "They're powerful."

"Hmm, some of 'em are, yeah. Some I only got to piss off my parents." He shrugs. "Call it a rebellious youth, or whatever."

"They're all hot to me," I bend to kiss the rose on his neck, enjoying the sharp inhale of his breath. I whisper, "And, one day, I'm going to trace every single one with my tongue."

"That'd better be a promise," he demands through decidedly

more ragged breathing. "You haven't seen my ass yet, either."

"For a Daddy, you're sounding a little bratty," I tease him, still whispering. I yelp when he swats at my bare butt, and my cock lurches at the sting.

"Don't go being bratty yourself, honey," he warns me. "I'm happy to spank you instead of blow you…and I promise that when it's a real punishment, you won't be allowed to come."

My heart picks up its pace and I hurry to agree. "I'll behave," I tell him. I'm not looking for a punishment today. "I'll be good, Daddy."

He squeezes the same butt cheek he just smacked. "Good boy."

How did I never know how much I needed to hear those words? Or is it just him and his decadent accent?

Eventually, we shuffle around on the mattress until we're both lying on our sides, with his dick in front of my face and mine in front of his. Having hastily discussed that we're both okay to go without condoms as we undressed, I wrap my left hand around his shaft, finally feeling the weight and warmth of him before I give him a couple of slow, experimental strokes.

I have had sex since Maddy died, but those first couple of times were a blur. This feels completely new to me — partially because it's with a new partner and isn't just a once-off fling, but also partially because it's been so long since I've been with someone so young. The skin of his legs has an elasticity and bounce that I'm no longer used to, as does the firm flesh of his perfect arse. I marvel at how smooth and tanned he is, how strong the muscles in his thighs are, and just how responsive his perfect cock is under my touch.

Then I finally duck my head to sample the bead of precum pearling on his purpled head and I don't know if it's him who moans, or me. Maybe it's both of us. He gives me time to explore slowly before I feel his breath ghosting over my own dick, and then I'm engulfed in the warmth and wetness of his mouth, taken to the back of his throat with an ease I can't replicate, and I don't know whether to thrust my hips or suck on the treat in my own mouth.

In the end, I just follow Oscar's lead. He starts to rock his hips and bob his mouth in an alternating movement that I echo, and it's not long before we're both moaning and grunting and gasping. If that weren't enough, his hands knead my ass, and I'm so distracted by how good it feels that I don't stop to think about how my body isn't anywhere near as toned as his. His dry fingers skirt into my crease and tease at my rim, prodding *just enough* to make me writhe, but not penetrating me.

I'm lost in a world of sensation, breathing in his musky scent as I suck on his cock, relishing the salty flavour of his precum and the feel of his girth against my tongue. Simultaneously, I fuck into his mouth, loving the heat and wetness around my cock, revelling in the slurping and moaning sounds surrounding us.

Once again, it feels like all-too-soon when my balls draw up tight, the building pleasure inside me coiling in the way that always precedes my orgasms. I moan loudly around Oscar's dick in my mouth, wondering if I should warn him, but he seems to just *know*, because he grips my arse and pulls me even further down his throat and then *swallows*—and that's it. That action does me in, sending me hurtling over the cliff, making me come so hard I see stars. I cry out, the sound of my bliss muffled by the thickness in my mouth. In a heartbeat, he groans and stills his hips, and his cock swells and then releases over my tongue and down my own throat, and I greedily swallow every drop, licking and sucking until he gently pulls away.

I feel boneless as I collapse back onto my pillow, still drifting in a haze of post-orgasmic endorphins. The bed shifts as Oscar turns himself back around, then he snuggles up to me, wrapping me in those deliciously tattooed arms.

"How are you feeling?" he asks me, his voice layered with the same sense of deep satisfaction settling into my bones.

"Wonderful," I answer honestly, then yawn.

He kisses my temple and kicks at the blankets until he's gotten them out from under us so he can pull them over our bodies. The days might be hot out here, but the nights can get a little chilly, and with the sweat on our skin cooling, I'm glad he had the energy to cover us before we pass out.

"Me too," he says, then adds. "Sleep, honey. We'll talk tomorrow about when I'm taking you out on that date."

"Hmm," I murmur sleepily, unable to keep my eyes open. "I don't remember agreeing…"

He snorts. "I can still spank you, darlin'."

"Don't threaten me with a good time, Daddy."

* * *

We wake up before dawn, something it seems we're both used to. What we're not used to, though, is the novelty of waking up in someone else's arms, or with someone else's morning wood nudging against us. Neither one of us has the willpower to stop when we start to kiss, morning breath be damned, and we rut against each other slowly, even as Oscar's second alarm goes off, warning him that he will be late for work.

"You shouldn't skip breakfast," I tell him, even as I'm closing my eyes to enjoy the feeling of his fist wrapping around both of our dicks.

"I'm...*fuck*...the Daddy, honey," he pants out, stealing a couple more soft kisses before adding, "I make the rules."

At this point, I've forgotten the point of whatever it was I was trying to argue. "Yes, Daddy," I agree, my own breathing turning ragged as his jerking becomes more frenetic.

I open my eyes to watch him for a moment, drinking in the blissful expression on his handsome face, finding the dusting of stubble over his jaw ridiculously attractive in the slowly dawning sunlight. Tell-tale jolts of pleasure start to travel through my nerve-endings, and my balls send up a warning that they're close. "Oh, fuck," I groan, "Fuck, fuck, fuck. I'm going to—*nnnngh*."

"*Fuuuuck*," he growls out, his release joining mine between our bodies, splashing over his fist and our bellies. He slams his mouth back on mine to ride out the final moments of our mutual orgasms, kissing me with an intense, possessive passion that has me wishing we could go again.

I'm lightheaded and breathing hard when we part, unable to stop sharing tiny, sweet chaste pecks to each other's lips in the afterglow.

"I could get used to waking up like this," I murmur, and he sighs happily.

"Me too."

Sadly, with him living on a station three hours' drive away from my vet practice, the likelihood of that happening is...not great. I don't put voice to the thought, though. Yes, the distance is going to be a problem, but not an insurmountable one. Not when the chemistry between us is this good.

Not when I can finally see myself being happy again.

And that is a simultaneously daunting and uplifting realisation to have as I hurriedly clean myself up and get dressed, ready for a long drive back to the new life I've been building for myself.

I just hope Oscar can really be a part of it.

Chapter Ten – Oscar

One of the many things I love about working for Rob is that he isn't one of those employers who runs his workers into the ground. He believes that happy employees are the most productive employees, so he gives us a fair, rotating roster, expecting us to work our asses off for two weeks, then we get one week off.

So, I spend the full week and a half following my night with Ryan balancing my usual long hours with texts and the occasional late-night call to my new boyfriend. I haven't taken him on a date yet, but I don't feel right calling him anything more casual than that. Not after the quality of the time we've shared together.

I don't just open up to anyone, and I get the feeling Ryan is the same. For whatever reason, we have connected with each other, and I feel like we could have something really special if we work for it.

And we do have to work for it.

It's difficult knowing that he's only a few hours' drive away while I have to work from dawn until dusk every day. But he's busy, too, doing calls to various farms and stations and also working with the domestic animals that are brought to his practice. It sounds like his business is booming, which is great, but it only adds to the list of reasons we can't see each other.

"I'm considering hiring another vet. Maybe someone fresh out of uni looking to learn the ropes on owning their own practice," he tells me over the phone one night as I lean against the outer wall of my bunk house. Dusty's snoring in his bunk inside, and it wouldn't be right to keep him up with my late-night conversation. "That's…how I met Maddy, actually."

"*Ohhh*," I tease, "was there some inappropriate boss/employee hanky-panky? How scandalous."

His laughter is rich and warm as it travels down the line and I wish I could see the matching joy on his face, to count the laughter lines in the corners of his pretty eyes and kiss his smiling lips.

Oh, man. I'm seriously gone for this Boy.

"No, nothing scandalous happened. Sorry to burst your bubble. I asked him out, we had dinner a few times, then we kissed for the first time…it was all very vanilla and above board, I'm afraid."

There's nothing vanilla about him now, though. I guess that came with time.

I make a show of sighing exaggeratedly. "Well, maybe I can come visit you at work on my days off and *we* can do some scandalous things in your office."

He's quiet for a moment, and I'm worried that I might have overstepped before his voice turns seductive and he asks, "What kind of scandalous things," he pauses, then adds,

"*Daddy?*"

I groan and, casting cautious glances to the left and right to ensure that I'm alone, palm my cock through my jeans. "You're not playin' fair, darlin'," I accuse, hearing the breathlessness in my own voice. "You know what you do to me."

"Maybe you should answer my question, then. Tell me what you'll do to me."

"Keep bratting me, honey, and I'll paddle your ass the next time I see you."

The low, drawn-out moan that rumbles down the line only makes me harder. "Oh, you like that idea, do you?"

"Fucking hell," he pants out. "Yes. Yes, I do."

"Hmm," I rub the heel of my palm over my straining erection, wishing I could do more, but I don't want to accidentally give one of the other guys a free show out here in the open, "maybe I need to think of a more suitable punishment, then. Maybe a cage? Restraints? Make you watch me jerk off without being allowed to touch —or come— yourself?"

He gasps and whines with every suggestion, but the last one has his breath hitching and a strangled keening sound meets my ears.

I still my hand on my pants and ask, "Sweetheart, did you just come?"

His silence is punctuated by heavy breathing.

I can't help but smile. "*Ryan,*" I press firmly, using my best Daddy Dom voice, "answer me."

"I…" I hear him swallow. "Yes, Daddy." Fuck, I can *hear* his embarrassment and my heart trips over itself.

He's so sweet and perfect.

"That's so hot, baby," I tell him, already planning on taking myself in hand when I get into my bunk. I commit the sounds he made to memory. "So, you like those ideas?"

"You know I do."

Oh, he gets sassy when he's embarrassed. It's adorable.

"Then I guess I'd better start planning my days off."

"Will you stay at my place for the week?"

I freeze at his question, not having expected the offer. I was planning on free camping in a local rest area, but the idea of sleeping beside him in his bed instead of on my own on a mattress in the back of my pickup is too nice to pass up. "I'd like that a hell of a lot," I answer carefully, "but only if you're comfortable with me staying with you."

"Oscar," all traces of playfulness are gone from his tone, "I call you Daddy. I'd say we're already way past that awkward early dating stage. I mean, I'm fifty-one and after Maddy…well, let's just say I don't want to play games and waste time beating around the bush. We're dating, right? And we're exclusive? So of course you're welcome to stay with me."

My heart squeezes again, and I nod, though he can't see me. "I love the way you think, darlin'."

In fact, I think I'm rapidly coming to love a lot more than that.

* * *

Ryan's home is wonderful. It's a two-bedroom, one-bathroom beachside villa, with the primary suite situated loft-style above the rest of the home, and the way he had described it over the phone really undersold how great it is.

Painted white with a blue roof, it gives off airy Greek island holiday vibes, not that I'd ever been out of the States before I came to Australia. From the back deck, there's an unimpeded view of white sand and crystal blue-green water. I drop my duffel bag on the white couch in the cosy living room and whistle as I slowly spin on the spot, taking it all in.

"You live in paradise," I admire.

"It's not *that* impressive."

"Rye, baby, it's a beach house. I always fantasised about livin' on a beach like this when I was a kid."

"You did?"

I turn to face him, wrapping my arms around his waist and looking him in the eye. "I did. But, I gotta say," I look around again, frowning, "I'm a little worried that you're a vet and you don't have any pets."

He snorts a laugh. "I work long hours. Some days, I'm only here for a few hours' sleep and then I'm gone again. That's not fair on a pet."

"Not even a turtle?"

"Not even a turtle," he answers with a sigh. "I'd love a dog, but it's not on the cards for me until I retire."

"What if you got a dog and took it with you to work and on house calls and stuff? I've seen vets do that."

He tilts his head from side to side. "That *is* an option…"

"And then you'd hopefully remember to eat properly because you've got to take care of another living creature, too."

Ryan stares at me for a moment, smiling widely, his tongue stretched into the corner of his lips, toying with the top row of his pearly white teeth. "You're *such* a Daddy," he eventually says, his tone bright and amused.

I kiss the tip of his nose then rub my own against it affectionately. "Guilty as charged. And, as your Daddy, I need to make sure you're lookin' after yourself when I'm not around."

"I've been looking after myself just fine."

"Uh huh." I raise an eyebrow and let him go, stalking over to his kitchen —which is basically just an L-shaped counter running along the back and side wall of the living/dining space— and open his gleaming, stainless-steel fridge. The contents are just as bare as I'd imagined, and I look back at him expectantly. "Let me guess," I drawl, "today's your usual grocery day?"

I shut the fridge door and open the freezer section on top. A wealth of frozen microwave dinners is stacked neatly on the top shelf.

"Baby," I sigh and pull out one that declares itself to be 'Spaghetti Bolognese'. I crinkle my nose at the package and slide it back on top of the pile, shutting the freezer door. "Those things ain't good for you."

"They're not—"

"This isn't up for discussion, darlin'. I know you're time poor, but your health is important to me. We'll come up with a compromise, but you're going to start eatin' right."

He bites his bottom lip, and I hold his gaze. Eventually, his lips twitch upwards into a tiny smile, and he nods. "Yes, Daddy."

"That's my good boy," I praise, loving the instant reaction it earns me. His skin flushes, and he shivers as his eyes darken with lust. Striding back over to him, I cup his jaw between my palms and kiss his lips. "Now, give me the rest of the grand tour."

Chapter Eleven – Ryan

I could get used to having Oscar in my house. I still have to work, but he spoils me by getting up early to make nutritious breakfasts, he packs me lunches, and there's dinner on the table when I get home. This week, I made an effort to schedule minimal visits outside of Denham, wanting to maximise my time with my boyfriend, and it has been so worth it.

It's been a long time since I've felt like I was someone else's priority, and I hope that Oscar can see that I'm making him mine, too. I know that right now things are new and shiny, and that we're in that exciting 'honeymoon' period of the relationship, but I feel like we have a genuine connection.

Our age gap still worries me, but with how mature Oscar is, I often forget that he's as young as he is. And he really does seem to only have eyes for me, even though he lives with a group of hot, young, queer men. I can't see the appeal in myself, but I can see that his attraction to me is genuine.

He's spoilt me for any other men, I muse as I shut down my computer on Friday evening, excited for the weekend ahead. I'm also dreading Sunday night, because that's the night Oscar will return to the station for his next two weeks of work.

"Big plans for the weekend?" Sarah asks me as we lock up together, making sure any of the medications are secured in the safes, along with any cash which missed the bank run yesterday.

Usually, I crack a joke about my wild party plans, but today I hesitate and blush, which catches my vet nurse's keen eye.

Her jaw drops and she blinks at me. "Holy shit, you actually have plans, don't you? *Romantic* plans," she adds as an afterthought, smirking at me knowingly. Then she reaches over and pushes my shoulder with her outstretched palm. "You sly dog: keeping all the juicy goss to yourself."

"Well, I'm not going to go spreading rumours about myself, Sez," I laugh.

"Yeah…you're not getting out of here without telling me all about your date, Doc." She folds her arms and tilts her blonde head, arching her eyebrows in a way that reminds me of Oscar. "Go on: spill. Name, age, occupation? How'd you meet? How's the sex?" She waggles her eyebrows as I splutter.

"Oscar. He's" —I clear my throat— "in his mid-thirties. He's a stationhand in Yalardy. We met…well, that's a long story, actually, but we met back in Brissie. I had no idea he was out here."

"Skipping the cradle-robbing for a moment," she teases, rolling her wrist, "you're skimping on the good stuff. The sex?"

"I'm not—"

"Ryan. Come on. Have you *seen* some of the straight guys around here? I'm living alone with my cats for the foreseeable future. Give me *something* sexy to work with."

"You really want to think of your boss having sex?" I ask her incredulously. "With another man?"

"Okay, scratch the straight men: have you seen *you*? Silver foxes are in right now, and you, my friend, are one of the foxiest."

"There are *so* many HR violations happening right now," I mutter, making her laugh.

"What HR?" Sarah asks me cheekily. "Do you need to report me to yourself, bossman?"

I groan. "I swear this is a lawsuit waiting to happen."

"I think we're good," she shrugs. "You're not the creepy old boss hitting on his young receptionist." Her smile fades away. "But if I am actually making you uncomfortable, I'll stop. I know I can be a bit full-on."

"I'm always uncomfortable talking about sex outside of..." I trail off, catching myself before I can give her more information about my private interests than necessary. "Anyway, no, you're not really making me uncomfortable. In fact, I've missed having friends to shoot the shit with. It's not as easy to do from the other side of the country."

"I'm glad to hear that," Sarah grins at me, looping her arm in mine as we leave the clinic, locking the doors and setting the alarms as we go, "because now that you've admitted that we're friends, you're gonna tell me *everything* about your new boy."

I snort. *I'm the Boy*, I think wryly, replying, "Ask your questions and I'll tell you what I can."

* * *

Dinner with Oscar on Friday night is fuelled by an undercurrent of excitement and anticipation. We get the bulk of the weekend to ourselves, barring any emergency calls, and from the moment I stepped across the threshold of my villa, the tension between us has been escalating.

I swear, Oscar has been deliberately teasing me with light touches and sweet, chaste kisses. He's edging me without doing anything overtly sexual, making me crave more of him with every brush of his hand over my shoulder or dusting of his lips over my cheeks and forehead.

Nothing even remotely flirtatious is said, though. We talk about my day and which animals I treated, then we switch over to Oscar's observations of the town and how much he enjoyed a lazy day spent sunbathing on the beach behind my house. From there we toss around plans for the weekend. It turns out the Shark Bay markets are happening on Sunday. We agree that it sounds like a fun event to explore, and if we want to spend Saturday in bed so we have the energy for a day out on Sunday…well, why not? At least, that's my logic, and I'm sticking with it.

"Or," Oscar laughs, sounding amused and indulgent after I make my suggestion, even as he carefully stacks our dishes into the dishwasher, "we can check out Shell Beach? I was reading about how unique it is and I kinda want to see it."

"You know, I haven't actually visited it," I consider, with a frown, feeling a bit like a bad local. I know I'm originally from Queensland, but I've lived here for a couple of months now and I should have made more of an effort to explore the surroundings of my new home. I pop the dishwasher tablet into its spot, shutting the lid for the compartment before shutting the front of the dishwasher.

"Then I guess that's settled," his tone is definitive, and it makes me smile. It eases some of the tension I didn't realise

I was carrying to have him make the decision for me. He smiles and continues, "I'd like to get some fish and chips and do the Aussie thing of eating 'em at the beach, too." Leaning in conspiratorially, he adds, "I haven't actually had any fish and chips since I've been here. In Australia, I mean."

"That's sacrilege," I sigh dramatically, shaking my head. "I guess I'll have to teach you, then, Daddy."

"I'm game for anythin' you want to teach me, darlin'."

Somehow, I don't think he's talking about food anymore.

* * *

Waking up together on Saturday morning without the pressure of either of us having to work is blissful. The sun filtering through the gaps around the blinds is already nearing uncomfortably warm, especially with Oscar wrapped around me like some kind of cuddly octopus, but I'm too comfortable and happy to mind. At some point during the night, we must have kicked off the sheets as they're tangled around our ankles, but I find I prefer being able to see the full expanse of Oscar's smooth, inked skin in the morning light.

My cock, already half-hard in its morning state, fills more as I drink him in.

A tiny pang of wistfulness hits me as I recall so many mornings like this spent with Maddy. I don't feel as though moving on is a betrayal or anything, and I know he would have wanted me to love and be loved again, the same way I would have wanted him to eventually find love if our roles were reversed, but I still miss him.

I know I'll always miss him, and that's okay. Oscar understands that. He would never ask me to hide or change that, either.

Besides, it's not that Maddy wouldn't have wanted me to grieve for him —because I know he would definitely have grieved me if I'd died before him— but he wouldn't have wanted me to spend the rest of my life alone.

Plus, I think as a smile curls my lips, *he would have thought Oscar was hot, too. He would have approved. Hell, he might have invited him to join us.*

Come to think of it, Maddy definitely would have approved of Oscar's Daddy Dom ideologies, too.

Oscar's dick twitches against my hip, pulling me out of my musings. "Mmm," he almost purrs, slowly sliding one tattooed hand down my furry chest and belly before wrapping it around my now very awake cock, "good morning, handsome." He leans back and then winks at me. "And good morning to you, too."

I chuckle, but the sound is cut off with a gasp as he starts to stroke me, using my precum for lube.

"Yes," he drawls, shifting his position so our faces are closer together, "a very good morning indeed."

"I've got morning breath," I warn him, and he shrugs without letting go of my cock.

"Don't care. I'm not minty-fresh either."

Then he's pressing our lips together and I forget all about my concerns, thrilling in this sweet, languid meeting of tongues and lips in the early morning hours. I wriggle my hand out from underneath him to reach in between our bodies, wanting to stroke him, too, and I grin against his mouth when he bucks his hips into my fist, the sticky wetness around his crown giving away how worked up he is, too.

Despite our instant chemistry, we've been taking things relatively slowly. We've jerked each other off, exchanged blow jobs and have frotted to orgasm a couple of times over the last few days, but he hasn't pushed to fuck me, and I haven't felt the need to go further, either. Until now.

Now, with no time constraints and nowhere to be, we have the time to do whatever we want. And I want him inside me. Reluctantly releasing his cock, I bring my hands to his firm pecs and gently push him until he's on his back. The lines of confusion between his eyebrows smooth out as I crawl over him until I'm straddling his hips, rocking mine so that our cocks slide together. I'm careful to balance my weight so I'm not putting it all on my knees, but his big, calloused palms grip the tops of my thighs, steadying me as I smile down at him.

"This is new," he says, sounding delighted. "Somethin' you want, darlin'?"

Rolling my hips again, I nod. "I think I'd like to...what's the saying? Save a horse and ride a cowboy?"

His dick jumps against mine while his fingers tighten on my thighs. "Yeah?" his question comes out breathily. "You got a particular cowboy in mind?"

"*Mmmhmmm,*" I lean forward a little, dancing my fingertips up the lines of ink on his hairless abs and chest. "There's a very sexy Texan in my bed. I think he'll do."

Oscar's head falls back into his pillow as he laughs. "Oh, he'll do, will he?" He swats at my bare butt, the sting of his palm meeting my flesh making me whine with pleasure. "Do you think bratty boys get what they want, honey?"

The playful words spoken so sinfully make my heart race. I bite my lip and widen my eyes. "I wasn't being bratty, Daddy. I was just trying to be cute."

"*Fuck,*" he drags the word out, his voice turning gravelly. "You're too perfect, darlin', you know that?"

Cocking my head, I press my luck, even as a cheeky smile tugs at my lips, refusing to be repressed. "Do perfect boys get what they want?"

Oscar's Adam's apple bobs. "You know you can have whatever you want with me, baby." Moving his palms, he rubs my thighs and then my knees. "You can handle this position without hurtin' yourself? Do you need pillows under your knees?"

This sweet, considerate man.

Swallowing back a lump of unexpected emotion, I nod again. "I can handle it," I answer, then add, "but pillows might still make it more comfortable."

"Good boy for bein' honest." The words make me shiver with pleasure, and he smiles as he grabs the two pillows from my side of the bed and gets me to lean and lift my knees one at a time as he gets the supports in place at his sides.

His hands move to my hips, then cup my bum, his fingers lightly teasing my crack. "Do you have lube, darlin'?"

Instead of answering verbally, I lean over to the bedside table—trusting his strong hands to prevent me from toppling over and onto the floor— and open the drawer, pulling out the first bottle I find and handing it to him as I right myself.

Oscar snaps the cap open and drizzles some onto his fingers, then pauses before clicking the lid shut again. He brings the bottle to his nose and sniffs at it, then reads the label. "Crème brûlée flavoured?" His tongue darts out to taste the viscous liquid on his fingers and he hums appreciatively, teasing, "And here I thought you were sweet enough already."

"I...um..." My cheeks burn as I recall why I bought the flavoured stuff to begin with. I'd had a fantasy of sucking a Dom off while fucking myself on a toy. Not having the energy or interest to actually go and find a Dom, I'd settled for spit-roasting myself between two toys. The flavoured lube had made sucking on the silicone cock more palatable.

"Oh, I'm gonna need to hear the story that has put that look on your face," Oscar tells me playfully. The next moment, though, he brings his lubed fingers to my hole, and I forget everything except the renewed desperate need to have him inside me.

"*Daddy...*" I whine, rocking my hips, trying to urge him to stop teasing and start fingering me. I don't even stop to consider how easily the epithet comes to me now.

"Be patient, honey. Let me enjoy this. It's our first time, and I wanna do it right."

If I wasn't so incredibly horny, I'd find that sentiment incredibly sweet. But I just want him inside me already!

"Please don't tease me," I beg, my eyes fluttering shut as two fingers finally breach me. It burns, but it burns *so good*. Gasping, I demand, "More, Daddy, more."

Scissoring his fingers, he gives me *almost* exactly what I'm craving. There's definitely a hint of pain to this stretch, but not as much as I imagine I'll get once I'm riding his perfect dick.

"Condom?" he asks when I start to bounce on his fingers, letting out a series of 'oh, oh, oh's alongside my moans of enjoyment.

I shake my head. When we got together at the station, we both disclosed our negative STI statuses, and we acknowledged that we're both on PrEP. Nothing has changed for me, and I trust that he'd tell me if anything had changed for him, too.

Still, I force my eyes open to look down at him and cautiously say, "Only if you want. I'm still good without."

"I am, too. Just checkin', though."

"I appreciate that."

And I do. Even though we're dating exclusively, we are still very new to each other. It means a lot that he takes sex as seriously as I do, and that he respects me enough to check in before we do anything new.

My thoughts are derailed as he removes his fingers and reaches between us to slick himself up. Then he holds his cock by its base and helps me to get into position so I can sink down on him and—

"Fuck, yes, baby," Oscar praises on a moan as my butt settles on the tops of his thighs, and I take a moment to relish the feeling of having him fully inside me for the first time.

"You feel so big, Daddy," I say and grind down, trying to get him as deep inside me as possible. "You're stretching me so good."

He grunts when I raise myself up and then drop down again, his fingers digging into the globes of my arse with almost bruising force. I love the additional ache and sting of it, the pain adding to the pleasure mounting beneath my skin.

I repeat my movement, picking up my pace as I start to bounce in earnest.

Oscar tilts his head back, rolling his hips underneath me. "That's it, darlin'. Ride me," he thrusts up, "*nngh, yeah*—just like that. You're such a good boy, ridin' Daddy's cock like a pro."

I'm babbling a new litany of 'oh, oh, oh's as I ride him, panting as a less-pleasant ache develops in my knees.

"D-daddy," I exhale, disappointed in my failing body, but knowing that he'll be upset if I hurt myself or withhold my discomfort, "m-my knees."

It's like a switch is flipped, and the arousal and enjoyment in his expression is replaced with concern. "On your back?" he asks, smoothing his arms up and down my sides. "Or do you need to stop?"

Stop? Abso-fucking-lutely not.

Instead of answering him, I pull him with me as I roll off him and onto my back.

He chuckles and adjusts his position, settling my legs around his waist, gentle and considerate of my sensitive joints. "Alright, no stopping. I got you, baby."

And he really, truly does.

Chapter Twelve – Oscar

Watching Ryan's face carefully for any signs of pain, I start to move again. I start off slowly, both because I want to ensure that I'm not hurting him, but also because I want to make this moment last.

The silence between us is broken only by our shared heavy breaths and gasps of pleasure, and the tiny smacks of our lips meeting when we can kiss between our pleasured exhalations. His ass grips me as I drag my cock in and out, and my balls send up their usual signals that I'm not going to last much longer.

"I need you to come for me, darlin'," I murmur, thrusting in a bit harder, following my body's instinct to chase down my own orgasm. "I'm gettin' close."

"Me too," he admits. His eyes are shut, and his face is lined with bliss. "I think…I think I'll come without you touching my cock."

"Fuck, that's hot."

"Mmhmm."

We kiss again as I rock into him with a bit more force, until he tears his mouth away, twisting his head to cry out, "Oh, yes, there! There, there, *there!*" I continue pumping into him, encouraged by his escalating cries and the scrabbling of his trimmed nails at my shoulder blades. "Daddy," he practically mewls, "Daddy, that's it. There. Again. Fuck. Daddy—*ungh!*"

His entire body tenses as he shudders through his orgasm, spasming around my cock until I go over the edge and release into his willing hole. I withdraw as I start to soften, collapsing onto the mattress beside him and snuggling up to him as we enjoy the afterglow together.

"I love it when you call me Daddy, darlin'," I tell him, feeling floaty from the endorphins. Pressing a kiss to the top of his sweaty head, I'm proud of myself for having the presence of mind not to declare 'I love you' like my gut is willing me to.

I've always been one to fall too quickly, and I'm trying to learn from my last sorry attempt at a relationship. But damn it if Ryan doesn't tick all my boxes and light me up from the inside just by being himself.

I'm fighting a losing battle against myself; one I'm finding that I'm happy to lose with the more I get to know my boyfriend.

My Boy.

He really is proving to be perfect for me in every way possible. This past week has proven that more than anything else could have. Ryan has soaked up every bit of affection I've offered him like a sponge. He has let me look after him, set him rules for looking after himself, and get to know him at his most relaxed. When he came home after a long, stressful day, I spanked him into subspace and then cuddled him to sleep afterwards. On days where that wasn't necessary, we've gone for evening strolls along the beach, or watched movies snuggled up on his couch.

I can see this becoming my future —our future— and that only makes me fall faster for him.

Nevertheless, I'm going to keep those three little words to myself for now.

His stomach rumbles, interrupting the moment, and we both laugh. "And there's our sign to get up and enjoy the day, hmm?"

He groans and covers his face with his pillow, then pulls the corner of it away to peek out one gorgeous grey-blue eye. "Breakfast in bed?"

I know before I even open my mouth that I'm going to give him anything he asks for, pushover Daddy that I am.

And it's the perfect start to a perfect weekend.

Chapter Thirteen – Ryan

After the amazing week we spent together, I'm on cloud nine. Sez teases me every time I smile down at my phone, and I can't deny that I probably look like a kid with his first crush. My heart certainly gives a flutter with every text and phone call Oscar and I exchange.

I still can't quite believe I've gotten so lucky. Not only did I find a Dom who isn't at all concerned by my body's limitations, but he's also a Daddy who wants to take care of me as well.

I'm well and truly beyond attached at this point. Which is why, during one of our evening phone calls, I get brave enough to ask, "Can I tell my kids about us?"

"Darlin'," I can hear the surprise in his voice, but I can also hear his smile, "you don't need my permission for that. You can tell them as much or as little as you're comfortable with. But," he clears his throat, "I'm real honoured that you want to tell them. I mean…" Oscar's tone turns cautious, "I'm the first person you've dated since their dad died, right?"

"You are," I answer him honestly and cross my feet at the

ankle over the top of my coffee table. "But they're adults. They're not going to get upset because I'm dating again."

Mak and Trev know more about my private life than most parents would be comfortable with, even considering their ages. But I've always been open and honest with them, and I've never been ashamed of being a Sub.

That said, I wouldn't know where to start in explaining that I call my new Dom 'Daddy'. *That* is something I might keep to myself for a while.

"That's not what I…" Oscar starts and then sighs. "I just…I know I've got big shoes to fill. Not that I'm replacin' Maddox. I don't ever want you to feel like I'm tryin' to do that."

I love how much thicker and more pronounced his accent gets when he's flustered.

"I know," I'm smiling as I assure him. "I'm not trying to replace him with you, either. Yeah, sometimes you remind me of him with the way you think, or the way you dom me, but…you're very different people and I love that you respect his place in my heart."

My eyes water and my nose tingles, but I manage to keep my voice steady. The last thing I want is for Oscar to think I'm upset. If anything, I'm getting emotional because of how happy Oscar makes me: something I honestly never thought I'd feel again.

"Well, fuck," he replies gruffly, clearing his throat, "now you got me tearin' up."

I burst into laughter, because I should have guessed he'd be on the same wavelength as me. Wiping away my own tears with the back of my hand, I thank him. Then I add, "So, I'm going to tell them about you."

"You gonna tell 'em how sexy I am?" he teases, and I can

picture his cocky smirk so vividly that my heart squeezes.

"I'll tell them I've gotten myself a real cowboy toyboy." I scrunch my nose. "Try saying that ten times fast."

He snorts before his voice dips into a low, seductive sort of growl, "There's only one Boy in this relationship, sweetheart, and it ain't me."

The reminder of how he sees me makes goosebumps erupt over my skin. Biting my lip even though he can't see me, I reply coyly, "Yes, Daddy."

"Fuck," he draws the curse out, curling his delicious accent around it in the way that's guaranteed to get me hard instantly.

I palm my cock over my pj pants. "Are you alone, Daddy?"

"I am," he answers. The cocky smirk is back in his voice. "Do you wanna have some fun on the phone, honey?"

Jerking off at his instruction isn't as good as having him here with me, but I agree enthusiastically anyway, and soon enough we're panting into each other's ears, egging each other on with a litany of 'yes's and 'that's it's and 'stroke harder's.

For once, he reaches the finish line before I do, and the sound of his raspy declaration that he's coming pushes me over the edge, too, until I collapse against the back of the couch bonelessly, not caring about the sticky mess inside my pants.

I laugh as I catch my breath, shaking my head at how ridiculous it is that our conversation derailed into sex so easily. I almost feel like a teenager again. I honestly can't complain about that.

"What?" he asks, sounding just as breathless and light.

"Just thinking about how good you are for me," I answer without any further explanation. Closing my eyes, I add, "I can't wait to tell Mak and Trev."

***

The kids take the news just as well as I'd anticipated. I had originally told them when I was going back out to the clubs again, brutally honest about my needs and my fears that I wouldn't feel right scratching my itches with someone who wasn't Maddy. Since then, they've both encouraged me to put myself out there, to find happiness and companionship, and they're both supportive when I tell them that I've met someone.

"I want to know all about him," Mak declares during the conference video chat we've established between the three of us. "What's his name? How did you meet?"

"Well," I lick my lips and watch as Trev's eyes narrow on the screen of my laptop. I prefer talking to them both this way, with a bigger screen than my phone can provide. I get to see their faces properly, which is nice because I miss them both terribly. "You remember how I said a Dom stepped in to help me when another Dom was…not treating me well?"

Yeah, I told them about that experience, too. Initially, it was because I'd still been reeling and had wanted Trev's perspective as someone familiar with criminal law. But, as I had rehashed it with them, I realised that I'd also wanted to tell them because I would want them to feel comfortable telling me such things if the tables were turned. As uncomfortable —and even upsetting— as it was to talk about, I'm glad I have such a close, open relationship with them. Their support also went a long way in helping me process what I'd gone through.

Trev blinks. "But…that happened in Brissie. Did you keep in touch with him? Your white knight?"

"He's more a cowboy than a knight…" I mutter before my brain can properly engage, and Mak laughs.

"So, that's a yes, then?"

"Actually, no." I really do enjoy telling this part of the story. It's like something out of a romcom. "By pure coincidence, we met again out at a cattle station in Yalardy. Turns out, he was just passing through Brissie in the end. Weird, right?"

Trev's gaze turns distant and there's the distinct clacking of keys from his end of the call. I watch him scrunch his nose. "Yalardy's like three hours from Denham," he says. "Isn't that a pain in the arse? Plus, he's a stationhand?" He looks at the camera with a frown. "Don't they work stupidly long hours and for weeks on end? How do you even date someone with that kind of schedule?"

"I swear to God, Trev," Mak sighs. "Can you not try to be positive? Papa's *happy* and you're being all—"

"It's fine," I cut in before they can squabble like children. I have the feeling they'll still bicker like five-year-olds even when they're in their eighties. "It's not like he's wrong. But," I smile, thinking about the amazing week I spent with Oscar, "his boss runs things a bit differently to most stations and we get to see each other for a week at a time every few weeks. It's working for us."

"Good," Mak's tone suggests that Trev had better agree with her or else. Then she smiles. "So…he's a stationhand. Does he have a name?"

Getting comfy in my seat, I sit back and prepare to babble happily about my boyfriend.

It's been a long time since I've felt this way, and I can only hope that it's a good indication of times to come.

Chapter Fourteen – Oscar

❦

It's not difficult to fall into a routine after that first visit to Ryan's place. While I'm working, I call, text and Facetime with him wherever possible, and on my weeks off, I drive to Denham and take up my role as his house-Daddy with pleasure. I fill his freezer with home cooked meals, though I do make an effort to take him on dates and spoil him as any good Daddy should, too.

In the privacy of his home, we also fall into a routine as Dom and Sub. Ryan craves the release and endorphins from regular discipline, and I love that he trusts me to meet his needs. It's not always spankings, either. As time moves on, we experiment with various toys like nipple clamps, floggers and whips, and I particularly enjoy edging him, adding to his frustration by introducing remote controlled vibrating plugs and chastity cages. I love making my Boy beg to come.

The guys at the station tease me about how smitten I am, and Ryan confesses that his colleague, Sarah, teases him just as much whenever she catches him smiling at his phone. It's nice to have that, I decide, even if I do threaten to kick Jim's ass every time I catch him making kissy faces at me. Back home, I'd come across a couple of guys who were also active in the BDSM scene, but there's something special about the group of men at this station.

It's like something out of a soap opera or cheesy LGBTQ romance novel: not the kind of set up you'd really expect to come across in real life. But every last one of the men I work with are somewhere on the queer and kinky spectrum, and they've become more of a family to me than the flesh and blood I left back in Texas.

Come to think of it, I should probably let my folks know I'm still alive out here, not that my pops would probably care either way. I was dead to him the moment I told him where he could shove his expectations of me. But Mama would care, even if our relationship is strained, courtesy of her being torn between wanting what's best for me and wanting to keep Pops happy.

When my phone rings in the middle of the day on a Thursday, four days away from my next week off, I frown when I see Ryan's name and smiling face on my screen. I take a moment to drink in the photo I took of him during our trip to Shell Beach, with the blue water sparkling behind him, contrasting with the white of the shells, the sunlight making his skin and smile even more vibrant. It's my favourite of all the photos we've taken together. But then I realise that he wouldn't be calling me on a workday if it wasn't important, and I hurry to press the green 'accept call' button.

"Hello?" I ask cautiously, stepping away from the fence I'd been mending. I pull my hat from my head and use it to fan myself in the heat of the midday sun. "What's up, darlin'?

Everything okay?"

"I…I'm being sued," he says, sounding like he's about five seconds from breaking down, and my frown deepens, both at the panic in his voice and at his words.

"Sued?" I repeat, dumbfounded. "For what? By whom?"

"For defamation by—hey, did you actually just use 'whom' correctly? Honestly, who says 'whom' in conversation? Been hanging out with the King of England or something?"

"*Ryan*," I bring out my Daddy Dom voice, trying not to smile at his questions. "Focus. Defamation? Why?"

He's quiet for a moment before he sighs. "The guy from The Vault. He's suing me for making that police report. Apparently, it caused damage to his reputation or character or whatever when they came to question him."

"His behaviour caused damage to his character," I growl, outright scowling at the reminder of the son of a bitch in question. Flashbacks of finding Ryan terrified and calling out for help churn my gut. I wish I'd turned around and planted my fist in that evil asshole's face. Even more so now that he's found a new way to torture my beautiful Boy. "Honey, he's not gonna get far with that lawsuit."

"But…"

"He's not. You've got witnesses. I'm a witness—"

"You're also my boyfriend, so a lawyer would argue… *something*. Spousal privilege? I don't know, I didn't study law."

"Okay, but I wasn't dating you when we met, and even so, there's the security guy—"

"Who didn't *see* anything." His voice breaks and my heart goes with it. "It's just my word against his."

I want to climb into my truck and drive to him, to comfort him and reassure him that the asshole who assaulted him isn't going to win here. But I can't. He's three hours away and I have to work. Then again, I'm sure Rob would give me some time off if I explained the situation to him. Even if he hasn't seen Ryan since the night that he helped Dusty over the phone, he's got a soft spot for my Boy, too, as anyone with half a brain should.

"Darlin', breathe for me," I try to soothe him over the line, my heart squeezing painfully again as he sniffles.

"Daddy," he says plaintively, "I can't deal with this."

"Yes, you can, baby. But I'm here and I'll help however I can."

* * *

After getting off the call, having been able to calm Ryan down enough to put off my instinct to run to his side, I start scrolling through my phone for contacts I never thought I'd have to use. My thumb hovers over the name Trevor Hatton for half a second before I press the call button and bring my phone to my ear.

When Ryan gave me his kids' numbers, it was with the understanding that I'd only ever contact them in case of an emergency, like if something happened to my Boy.

This counts, right?

Ryan's sniffles echo in my brain, and I set my jaw. It counts, all right.

The line rings a couple of times before a pleasant voice answers, "Trevor speaking."

"Hi," I start, "my name's Oscar Williams. I'm—"

"Papa's boyfriend," he finishes for me. His tone turns sharper. "What's happened? You wouldn't be calling me out of the blue in the middle of a workday just to introduce yourself."

Smart guy, I think to myself, nodding. "Rye's fine. Well, physically speaking," I assure him. "But he's being sued for defamation by…" I trail off, suddenly unsure of myself and this decision I've made to enlist Ryan's stepson's help. Because the guy might be a lawyer, but he works in criminal law and, by doing this, there's a possibility I'm going to give away information Ryan might have been keeping to himself.

"Defamation?" Trevor sounds as bewildered as I felt, but after a beat he says, "Don't tell me it's got something to do with the lowlife he reported to the police before he left Brissie. I know Papa doesn't tell us everything, but that's the only thing I can think of…"

I knew that Ryan was close to the kids he'd helped raise —close enough that they call him 'Papa', even as adults— but I didn't realise they shared quite so much information with each other. But it's a relief to learn as much, because it means my fear of accidentally outing Ryan's kinkier side to his kids has been allayed.

"Yeah, you got it in one," I tell him. "Rye's beside himself, and I'm pissed that this guy even thinks he has a case. I mean, as far as we knew, he hasn't even gone to trial or anythin' for the charges yet, assuming he's even been charged at all."

In fact, I only suggested the other day that Ryan should reach out to the police back in Brisbane to see what had happened with the report he'd filed. He just assumed that there hadn't been enough evidence, despite our witness statements, and that was that. At least filing a report means that there will be evidence of the guy's behaviour if someone else steps forward in the future, but I was secretly hoping the guy would pay for what he'd done to my Boy.

"Well, *that* is a criminal issue I can help with, but the

defamation suit is a civil matter," he replies after a moment of contemplation. "Hold on a tic," I hear the distinct sound of typing and then he says, "Okay, so, I can't help with a civil suit, but I'm sending a friend from uni an email. Henry specialises in family law now, but this will still be in his wheelhouse. He's based on the Gold Coast, but he'll take meetings via Facetime and will happily travel when need be. Can I give him your number in case Papa's in surgery or can't get reception?"

"Yeah, of course."

"Excellent." There's more tip-tapping of keys in the background of the call, before Trevor says, "Okay, sent. And I'll call Papa later to let him know, too. I'm pretty sure Old Mate hasn't got a leg to stand on —Papa's got a defence under the argument of fair reporting at the very least— but Henry will be better equipped to go through it all with you guys."

I'm relieved to hear it, and I thank him profusely, adding, "I'm sorry that this is our first time talking. I really, uh, care about Ryan," I love him, actually, but I haven't told him yet, so it feels wrong to say it to anyone else first, "and you and your sister mean the world to him. And I'm sorry for your loss, too. Your dad sounds like he was a great man."

There's another extended moment of silence before Trevor says, "He was. And thank you. It sounds like you're a good guy, too." He pauses, and even on the other end of the line I can feel a subtle change of tension in our conversation. I guess what's coming next before he adds, "I hope you're not all talk, Oscar. You'd better be treating my Papa right."

"I promise I am."

"Good." A smile seems to lift his voice. "Thank you for calling me. I appreciate it."

Winding up the call, I debate texting Ryan to let him know

what I've done, but then I decide to call him back instead, just in case I've overstepped. I'm his Daddy, and I promised him that I'd try to take on a lot of his stresses and hard decisions as part of that, but this is his first time being someone's Boy, and communication is still key to making this work.

"You really called Trev?" he asks me after I've given him the update, and I can't quite read his tone. He doesn't sound upset, but he does sound a bit wobbly.

"I did," I fan myself with my hat again, cursing the heat and lamenting the extra time I'll take fixing the fence. But Ryan is more important right now, and Rob will understand that. "Is that okay?"

My heart seizes just a little as his breathing hitches, but then he answers, "Oscar…*Daddy*, it's better than okay. Thank you."

Oh, thank God.

Ryan continues, oblivious to my sudden sense of overwhelming relief, "I had no idea where to start, and I…I felt stupid about it." I don't like the self-deprecation in his tone. "I'm almost fifty-two-years-old, and I just—I just panicked. I've never been sued before. I didn't even think to call my own kid."

"That's a perfectly understandable response," I soothe, wishing yet again that I could just bundle him into my arms and hold him until he feels better. "And I'm glad you don't think I crossed a line. You're my Boy, and I promised I'd take care of you. I know I should have asked you if it was okay first, but I didn't think of calling Trevor until after our call ended." Then I just acted on instinct.

Impulsive, I chide myself. *That's what landed you here to begin with.*

Not that it's a bad thing that I am. In fact, coming to Australia is still the best decision I've ever made, even if things have turned out quite differently to what I had originally anticipated. Some might argue they've turned out even better this way. They'd be right.

"We might not have considered this situation specifically, but I meant it when I said I trusted you to make important decisions for me," he reminds me gently, and now I wonder which one of us is supposed to be comforting the other. "This is part of that. It means a lot to me that you reached out to Trev, and I'm glad that I don't have to go looking for a lawyer now. It's a weight off my shoulders. A huge weight, actually. So, yeah. Thank you, Daddy." He goes quiet for a beat before he says, "Can I…I mean, would Rob let me hire a cabin for a few nights? I, um, I'm going to cancel my appointments for the next couple of days and…I really just want to be close to you. It's okay if you have to work, but—"

"Rob ain't gonna take your money," I tell him with certainty, more than excited by the prospect of seeing him tonight after all. Of being able to hold him close and see for myself that he's really okay. "But there'll definitely be a cabin here for you, honey. Leave that to me and drive carefully, all right?"

Ryan promises that he will, and we say goodbye again. Cringing at the mess of fence posts and wire I still need to deal with, I bring Rob's contact details up on my screen and call him next.

Come hell or high water, I'm taking care of my Boy first.

Chapter Fifteen – Ryan

Wombat Run Station is a sight for sore eyes. I've only been here once before but pulling up to the main gate and its logo which is far too cute for a cattle station, but is somehow perfect for the men behind these brick and iron walls, fills me with a sense of home and belonging so strong that my eyes well with tears. Dusty's the one to meet me this time, greeting me with a jovial wave before he opens the gates and gestures for me to drive through.

There's just something special about this place. A lot of it is the people, I'm sure. They're all so welcoming and nonjudgemental; something I've come to fully appreciate in the months since Oscar and I started dating. Hearing his stories about their shenanigans assures me that I can embrace my Daddy with open arms and even call him by that title without any of these stationhands so much as batting an eye.

It's not just the people, though. The place itself is warm and inviting. The long, gravel driveway leads up to the main farmhouse, which looks like something out of a TV show or movie. It's a high-set single storey Queenslander-style house; timber in construction with a wrap-around veranda and a corrugated roof. The outer façade is painted a mossy green colour, and all the balustrades, support beams and window trims are bright white. It's just so *country* and welcoming.

The paddocks and fields around the property are vast, and while they're not all lush and green (not with the Western Australian sun bearing down on them all year around), there's still something idyllic about the stretches of reddish brown dirt and grass which has faded to almost a wheaten colour.

The sky overhead is clear and stretches on forever and is currently turning magenta and pink with streaks of orange as the sun begins to set — a spectacular view which is only enhanced by the fluffy white clouds drifting over the horizon.

You just don't get views like this in the city.

Admittedly, I get wonderful ocean sunset views from my little villa on the beach, but there's something extra spectacular about watching the sun setting over the seemingly never-ending paddocks at the station.

Then there's also the scents in the air. It smells like a farm, with cattle and horses and grass, but the air is fresh and crisp, even in the dying heat of the early evening. I find it invigorating and soothing all at once, even if I am technically a born and bred city boy.

Maybe I'm a reformed city boy? Reforming, even?

My train of thought is derailed as the front door of the main house swings open and Rob steps out, beaming down at me from the top of the front steps. "Doc!" he greets jovially, making an ushering movement with his arm, "Come on in. Let's get you a drink."

"Just water's fine," I tell him, and he scoffs.

"After the day you've had, plus that drive? At least have a beer with me." Then he stops in his tracks and grimaces, shifting to apologetic as he goes on, "Unless you don't drink alcohol. The boys keep telling me I need to stop just assuming everyone does."

"It's all good," I shoot him an easy smile. "I do drink occasionally…mostly socially, to be honest…but I'm usually more a red wine guy, or I'll have a good quality bourbon over ice."

"I can arrange either of those things."

"Maybe later." I wipe my feet on the welcome mat before I step onto the polished timber floors inside. "How's Jemima doing? And Little Ted?" Cocking my head, I move to turn back to the door. "Want me to check in on them? Or any other animals while I'm here?"

"All the animals are doing just fine," Rob places his hand on my shoulder and redirects me towards a generously sized living room, "and you're not working while you're here. Ozzy would have my head if he thought I was taking advantage that way."

I snort. "You're his boss, and you're doing me a huge favour letting me crash in one of your cabins for a couple of nights. The least I can do is—"

"Nuh-uh. You're a guest here, Doc, and your money isn't any good here, either, just before you start getting any ideas." He guides me into a cushy brown leather armchair. "Besides, he's your Dom, not me. He'd have every right to take me to task if I put you to work."

I blink. "How'd you—"

"Most everyone here's some kind of kinky," he shrugs and drops into the chair beside mine, "and we're all pretty open about our interests. I know Ozzy's a Daddy Dom, so it goes to reason you're his Sub."

"His Boy," I admit quietly, not having spoken the words aloud to anyone other than Oscar himself. "I'm—I'm his Boy, actually."

Rob's knowing grin widens and he nods. "I'm happy for you both." He leans forward, then conspiratorially says, "I've put you in the honeymoon cabin. It's a bit further out than the rest, and I'm giving Oz tomorrow off as a personal day."

My cheeks flame at the suggestion underlying his words. "Oh, no, I just needed—"

"Your Dom to take care of you," he finishes firmly, giving me a stare that almost dares me to argue with him. "Let Ozzy take care of you, Doc," he continues in a gentler tone when I don't press my luck. Every bit of my submissive nature refuses to. I've never really been a brat, and I won't be starting with a strange Dom, no matter how fair he seems. "I've made sure there's food up in the cabin, too, so you don't have to face the rabble here."

I fight back the overwhelming urge to hug him. Throat tight, I force out a gruff, "Thank you" which doesn't cover half the gratitude I feel at his understanding and compassion.

If I can be half the boss and friend that this guy is, I'll be doing alright.

"There you are," Oscar's voice comes from the archway leading to the main foyer and just the sight of him relaxes me. He strides across the living room with his gaze locked on mine, not even acknowledging his employer before he stands in front of me and then pulls me up from my seat and into his strong hug.

He smells freshly showered, his signature coconut and lime

bodywash tickling my nose as I press my face into the crook of his neck. *Daddy*, I think almost desperately. *Safe.*

It should be startling that I've come to think of this young man as my safe space, but we've gotten close over these past few months, and I believe Maddy would be relieved to know that I'm not alone anymore.

"Oh, darlin', I've got you," he murmurs soothingly, his hand rubbing up and down my spine, and I'm surprised to realise that I'm shaking. "You can let go. I'm taking over now."

Just like that, the last of my worries fade away. I trust that he will follow through on his pronouncement. The fact that he took the initiative to call Trev and organise a lawyer for me while I was still melting down over the letter I received this morning means more than I can properly express. He knew exactly what I needed, and he took care of it. Took care of me. He's going to do the same thing now, and even if I don't know exactly what I need, I trust that he will.

* * *

"Sit," Daddy demands once we're in the cabin, with him having pried me out of the main house with his own thanks issued towards Rob. He gently nudges me onto the loveseat in front of the unlit fireplace. "I'll sort out a light dinner because I'm guessing you haven't eaten, and then we'll talk."

I scrunch my nose. I don't want to talk. I want to be draped over his lap and spanked into subspace. I want him to paddle my arse red and raw, until I'm sobbing and letting out all of my pent-up emotions. I want pain and release.

"We're not going into a scene until I know you're really okay to." His tone is a strange mix of empathetic and commanding.

"So, food then talking. After that, we'll take things as they come. Understood?"

As much as I really need the release, I do appreciate that he's putting my mental and physical health first. "Yes," I nod.

He arches an eyebrow. "Yes *what*, Ryan?"

Straightening my spine, I allow the shiver of pure arousal to travel through me at that firm, serious tone. "Yes, Daddy."

Oscar smiles. "Good boy. Now, try and relax and I'll throw a quick dinner together."

He rummages around in the kitchenette, pulling things out of the fridge and the cupboards as he quite literally throws together a salad with some grilled chicken and a vinaigrette dressing. We eat at the little two-seat dining table and then settle back on the couch together after he washes the dishes, allowing me to dry them.

I have to admit, I'm feeling significantly better for having eaten and exchanged small talk over our meal. I've still got stress and anxiety itching under my skin, but I don't feel close to breaking down anymore. Daddy looks relieved when I tell him so.

"Good," he says softly. "I'm happy to give you the relief you need, but I won't ever do it if you're too far gone in your head to give proper, considered consent. I need to know that you'll still safe-word if things go too far, you know?"

How could he have ever doubted himself as a Daddy or a Dom?

"Thank you, Daddy. That means a lot to me." He's got my best interests at heart, and that only solidifies my trust in him.

It also reaffirms my love for him.

Before I can open my mouth to tell him that, he asks me, "What do you need tonight, darlin'?"

I think about how deeply I trust him. About how intimate I

need my punishment and release to feel. The answer comes to me easily, though it's not something I've let anyone other than Maddy do to me before.

Licking my lips, I raise my chin and look him in the eyes, knowing that this isn't something I can appear hesitant to suggest. He has to know how serious I am.

"Choke me, Daddy." I watch the surprise on his face, and I press just a bit harder, "Choke me and fuck me hard. I want to feel you for days."

Chapter Sixteen — Oscar

My heart is racing.

Ryan's asking —no, *begging*— for me to choke him and I am so torn right now.

On one hand, I'll give my Boy anything he needs. On the other, choking is always dangerous, especially if you haven't studied the anatomy of a person's neck and head. I've rarely indulged in any kind of asphyxiation play — not because I haven't studied and practiced the safest ways to do it, but because it takes a level of trust between partners which I've never really had.

Until now.

"I need it rough, Daddy," he adds, almost sounding plaintive now. Then he goes in for the kill, placing his hand on my thigh and confessing, "I trust you."

Fuck me.

"I've got you, darlin'," I practically coo, wrapping my hand around the back of his neck and squeezing to let him know that I'm on board. "But we're setting some ground rules first."

"That's fair," he acknowledges with a nod.

"Good. So, I need to know your actual limits. I know you say you need it rough, but what do you consider rough? A hand to your neck? Mild squeezing? Cutting off your air supply?"

"Squeezing," he answers. "Cutting off my air, but…not for long."

"Okay. You'll need to give me a cue on when to stop." I consider the few items I brought with me in my overnight bag. "I've brought a bell with me. I'll get you to hold it through the scene. Shake it when you need me to ease up on squeezing, drop it if you need to safe-word. Does that sound fair?"

"Yes, Daddy."

"Good boy."

"I'd also like your hand to guide me, at least this first time. So, the hand that isn't holding the bell is going to sit over the top of mine and direct my movements, all right? If you forget to shake the bell, you can pull back on my wrist to get me to ease up."

He takes a moment to consider this and then nods. "Yeah, that…that makes sense, actually."

I'm glad to hear it. After running through the rules again, and explaining that I will be stopping to check in with him as we go, we get ourselves ready for the scene.

I enjoy watching him strip for me, instructing him to do it slowly and to carefully fold his clothes and set them aside neatly. This not only draws out his anticipation, but also settles him back into a more submissive frame of mind. By the time he's lying back on the mattress, naked and spread out for me, I've also taken off my clothes and dropped them onto the couch. I've got the bell I told him about ready and waiting, and a small bottle of lube on the nightstand.

"What's your colour right now, honey?" I ask as I crawl over him, watching him for any signs of hesitation.

"Green," his answer is confident. "I need this, Daddy. I trust you."

"Okay," I hand over the bell. "Give that a shake for me. Make sure it works."

Ryan complies, and the tinkling sound is perfectly loud enough for us to hear, even with his fist closed around the bell. Nevertheless, I remind him again that he can also pull my wrist away from his throat if he needs me to loosen up, or he can drop the bell to safe-word.

"Yes, Daddy," he agrees dutifully and it's all I can do not to kiss him.

He's too perfect.

"Good boy."

I reach for the lube and coat my fingers, and Ryan spreads his legs for me without needing to be asked. However, when I rub his rim, he arches his back and says, "Don't…don't prep me. I want your cock to open me up."

"You sure?" I mightn't be the biggest guy around, but it'll still hurt.

"*Please.*"

I can't deny him anything.

Slicking up my cock, I slowly push inside him, groaning at how tight he is. I'm almost afraid that he's too tight and too tense, but after a moment, he relaxes a fraction and it's enough for me to continue.

He's panting against the intrusion, his eyes clenched shut and his chest rising and falling rapidly. Once I'm all the way in, I check in.

"Colour?"

"G-green. Fuck, you feel huge. But d-definitely —*nnngh*— green. Now move." He hisses in a breath. "Please."

I rock back and forth in short, almost agonizingly slow moments. He's gripping my cock like a silken vise, and if I'm not careful I'm going to come before we've even started.

Eventually, we hit a steady rhythm, and his whines move from pained to pleasured.

Distracting myself from my impending orgasm, I brace my body over his on my left arm and reach for his throat with my right, resting my hand gently around it. Just touching, not even holding on. His eyes fly open and lock with mine, and I note that the grey tint in them is more pronounced and stormier than usual, his pupils blown wide with lust.

"Colour?" I ask softly.

"Green, Daddy," he whispers back. "Do it. Choke me."

"Hand over mine, honey. That's it," I add as he does as he's told. "Good boy."

Still staring into my eyes, he starts to squeeze my hand with his, guiding me to apply pressure to the sides of his throat. It's still not enough to impede his breathing or blood flow, but his eyes seem to get darker with desire anyway.

"Colour?"

"Green."

He squeezes my hand more firmly, and I tighten my hold on his neck. This time, his breathing hitches into a raspy little gasp, and his eyes flutter shut. Still rolling my hips, I keep my hold for a couple of extended seconds before easing up, and he whines.

"More," Ryan urges, "*harder.*"

"The fucking or the choking?"

"Both!" He arches his back, "Please, Daddy?" He tries to

clamp down around my hand, and I shake my head.

"*Tsk-tsk,*" I chide, teasing him with the slow drag of my cock in and out of him, "we're takin' this slowly, darlin'."

He huffs but doesn't argue. He's too submissive and nowhere near bratty enough to literally force my hand. Instead, he whines again. "Please?"

Damn it, but I'm gonna fall for that pretty pleading every single time.

I thrust into him with more intensity, delighting in the much louder gasp the action forces out of him. Then I squeeze the sides of his neck again, careful not to put any pressure on his trachea, applying a bit more force than last time as I thrust back into him again and again. I manage three quick, hard slams of my hips before I release my hold again.

"Colour?" I pant.

"Green. So…*oh, fuck*…so much green." His voice has taken on a bit of a rasp, and the sound of it travels from my ears and to my cock.

I choke him some more, loving the feeling of his hand applying tight pressure over the top of my own, and the incredibly tight grip his clenching ass has on my dick. Ryan's face is flushing from the restricted air and blood flow, and potentially also from his arousal. Easing up my hold again, his eyes roll back with pleasure and he moans.

Bingo.

We've found the sweet spot for him, where the dopamine and serotonin have begun to do their thing.

"*More,*" he encourages.

I squeeze the sides of his throat with a similar amount of pressure as before, slamming my cock inside him once, twice, three times. After checking in once more, we do it all over again. And again. And again.

He's starting to make sharp, gasping sounds as I fuck him, unable to take in enough breath to properly let them out. It's hot as fuck, as is the purplish tint to his face. He's sweaty and crying and thoroughly wrecked, and when I release my latest hold from around his throat, he arches off the mattress with a choked cry. I'm barely cognizant of the fact that he's coming all over my abs and his own belly because I'm coming, too, my cock unable to take the even tighter clenching of his ass as his body tenses during orgasm.

His hand slips from mine, his entire body lax beneath me. Ryan's eyes are glazed over in the familiar way which suggests he's hit subspace. I withdraw from him carefully and spread out beside him, cuddling him to me, heedless of the mess of cum and sweat between us.

Pressing soft, gentle kisses to the top of his head, I splay my hand over his chest and focus on the thumping of his racing heart as it begins to gradually slow down. Eventually, just when I think he's slipped from subspace into sleep, he stirs and sniffles against the remnants of his emotional release. The bell tinkles as it drops against the mattress, unnecessary and forgotten.

"Hey darlin'," I murmur, gently kissing his sweaty hair again, "welcome back. How are you feelin'?"

He snuggles against me and hums. It's a contented sound. "So much better. I needed that." He pauses, then quietly adds, "Thank you."

"It was my pleasure and privilege, honey," I reply seriously. "Thank you for your trust." Before the moment can get too emotional, I ask, "Was that all good for you? Highlights? Things you'd change?"

I cringe as the awkwardly phrased questions tumble out of me, taking me all the way back to my days in training to be a Dom. But what we just did was *huge* and I'm a little shaken by how emotional I feel after our session.

"It was perfect," Ryan answers easily, tilting his head back so we can look at each other. "Highlights were obviously when the dizziness and pleasure kicked in, but I needed the pain, and I knew you had control of the situation. There wasn't any panic or fear. But next time…" He trails off and nibbles at his abused lower lip.

"Next time?"

"You can go harder. I trust you. I" —he takes a deep breath— "I love you, Oscar."

And, just like that, the shakiness of my emotional state lifts, leaving me with absolute certainty. "I love you, too, Ryan."

Chapter Seventeen — Ryan

Oscar didn't need to say the words for me to know how he feels. I saw it in his eyes during our session, felt it in his determination to give me what I'd asked for as safely as possible, and had it confirmed in his gentle questioning during his aftercare.

I watch in comfortable silence as he climbs out of bed to get a wet washcloth, then lie back as he wipes me clean, giving himself a scrub with the same cloth once he's satisfied that I'm good. Then he tosses the cloth into the bathroom and pads over to the kitchenette, reaching into the fridge and emerging with two bottles of water. One of them, he sets down on the bedside table. The other, he cracks open and passes to me as he climbs back into bed, snuggling against my side again.

I drink greedily from the plastic bottle, relishing in the condensation that wets my fingers. My body is still heated and sweaty, and I feel like a shower is in order, but I don't want to break the softness and sweetness of this moment.

After draining half the bottle, I twist the cap back on and drop it unceremoniously on my bedside table, turning over so I can plaster myself to Oscar's toned, tattooed flesh. I kiss whatever skin I can reach. It's not because I'm trying to be sexual, but because I can't resist the sensation of his skin beneath my lips.

His arms, strengthened by his manual work, wrap around me like the sexiest of cocoons. I can feel the steady rhythm of his heart beating against my own, and I feel at home in a way I haven't since Maddy died.

I'm loved. Taken care of. Protected from the world.

"We should probably shower before we fall asleep like this," Oscar eventually says, and I smile into his shoulder.

"Oh, is showering with me a chore?" I ask playfully, and he swats at my bare backside.

"Stop pretending you're a brat, honey. We both know you're not."

I snort. "Maybe I'm trying something new. I've never been a Boy before, either." I lean back and bat my lashes at him exaggeratedly. "You'll still love me if I'm bratty, won't you, Daddy?"

Oscar laughs and groans all at once. "This post-subspace high is adorable," he declares, but then his expression softens. "But I love every version of you there is, darlin'."

If I hadn't already fallen in love with him, that would have done it.

* * *

Staying at the station is everything I needed and then some. Leaving the stress of work and life behind, knowing that Oscar will take care of me in every way I need, was the right choice to make. Even though I agonised over closing the practice, I knew that I wasn't going to be in the right frame of mind to be treating patients — especially when the patients can't verbalise their issues.

Knowing that Sarah's going to send any emergency calls on to the closest vets she can, I'm happy to let my Dom —my Daddy— make every other decision for me.

And he does.

He decides what we're eating and when. He decides when we're going to go for a walk down to the petting zoo, and when we're going to take a nap curled together on top of the bed's crumpled white quilt. He also decides that I don't need a spanking or a paddling, and I have to admit that I'm still feeling settled after the intense emotional release from being choked, so I don't push the issue.

It's perfect.

It's all perfect.

I can't remember the last time I felt like I took a holiday. If I strain my memory, I realise that it was before Maddy died. Afterwards, the year I spent trying to regain my equilibrium felt more like purgatory than anything else, even though I wasn't working. I'd been grieving and lost and alone.

I'm none of those things anymore.

Yes, I will always grieve Maddy, but he would have hated to see me wasting away, not taking proper care of myself or even attempting to find happiness. I don't believe in an afterlife, nor am I at all religious, but every so often, I like to think that I can feel his approval in my choice to move on.

Having his kids' —our kids'— approval helps, too.

Calling to tell them that I was dating again was one of the most awkward things I've ever done, but both Mak and Trev assured me that they wanted to see me happy. Mak even said she was relieved to know I was trying to find love again. Neither of them pushed me for any more information than I was willing to give and, while I had hinted that Oscar is a bit younger than me, I haven't told them how much younger.

I guess I'm still afraid that they'll be weirded out that I'm dating someone barely older than they are.

And while they know that their Dad and I were into BDSM (courtesy of their teenage selves snooping in places they shouldn't have been), I honestly don't know how well they'd take it if they heard me calling Oscar 'Daddy'.

Not that he's ever asked me to do so in front of other people. I'm sure he'd love it, but he also understands how new the dynamic is for me, and probably also how I'm afraid people might react.

So, all that to say, I'm happy now. I'm finding my way, and I'm not alone.

I've achieved a lot of that on my own, I know I did. But finding Oscar made everything so much better. He came into my life at just the right time, and he hasn't so much as batted an eyelid at my issues. Even now, with my withdrawal from life because of a simple civil lawsuit, he's staying strong and helping me through it.

He even sits with me through the initial phone call with Henry, the lawyer Trevor set me up with.

We're at the tiny little table in the cabin, and I've got my phone propped up on the table so we can meet with Henry via Facetime. Oscar squeezes my hand in full view of the camera. Henry smiles warmly at us as he introduces himself, and I acknowledge that we did actually meet at Maddy's funeral: a bunch of Trev and Mak's friends came as emotional support, but the whole day is still a blur to me.

"I'm still sorry we're not properly meeting under better circumstances," he says smoothly, and his youthful dark skin crinkles at his forehead as his expression pulls into a frown, but then his words immediately surprise me, "I've reached out to the claimant's lawyer and, to be honest, even he thinks his client's case is shaky at best. I advised him that we will be arguing your civil rights under Section twenty-nine of the Defamation Act to make a fair report. I could also argue justification under Sections twenty-five and twenty-six of the Act due to the nature of the statements being both substantially true and contextually true, however I know he'll contest that the case hasn't been tried in a criminal court, so his client hasn't been found guilty…but that still doesn't negate your rights to make the report in the first place."

"So, what you're sayin'," Oscar cuts in while my panicked brain tries to catch up, "is that his lawyer is aware that he ain't got a leg to stand on."

"Correct," Henry nods. In the little video feed, he clasps his hands together on the surface of his desk. "The best they can do is try to argue that you knowingly made a false report with the intent of injuring his reputation."

"Which he damn well did not!" Oscar's temper flares, and it's such a rare thing to hear him raising his voice in anger that I startle a little.

He immediately squeezes my hand a bit tighter and grimaces. "Sorry, darlin'. It just grinds my gears to think that someone would say those things about you."

I nod and squeeze his hand right back. "I know. But," I smile shyly, forgetting our audience, "you're hot when you're angry."

Henry clears his throat, and I blush and look back at the phone screen. He looks thoroughly amused. "You remind me of some friends of mine," he says, then gives himself a little shake and settles back into work mode. "The old 'he said/he said' stuff is where we might have an issue. However," he starts flicking through the manila folder which had been sitting untouched in front of him, "the police took statements from the club during their investigation, and they included character references. The fact that you were a regular and an 'ideal patron' and he was new to the scene works in your favour. And they recovered video footage of the hallway leading to the private rooms which appears to corroborate your report."

So then why hasn't he been charged? Sentenced? Locked up so he can't do it to someone else again? I wonder bitterly.

Oscar doesn't have my restraint, and he asks the question out loud: "If they've got all this proof, why the hell isn't he in jail yet?"

Henry sighs. "Probably a number of factors. Due to the situation, you understandably reported the incident after the fact, and there wasn't any physical or DNA evidence to collect. It took the CIB —the Criminal Investigation Branch— some time to begin their investigation beyond your initial statements, and a while longer to locate your assailant. His statement would have contradicted yours, and then they have to investigate further to prove that he's lying. It's not as cut and dry as TV makes it look. But, obviously, just being questioned by the police was enough to spook the guy and set off this whole absurd lawsuit against you."

"Which you think won't go anywhere?" Oscar prods with a frown.

Henry nods. "I know it won't. In fact, I don't even think you need to travel back here to attend any mediation sessions. We can do it by Facetime or Zoom or whatever if we absolutely have to."

Oscar hums thoughtfully. "What about the criminal charges? What happens there?"

"I'm not specialised in Criminal Law" —on the screen, Henry closes the manila folder and leans forward over the top of it "—but this won't derail that as much as he probably thinks it will. The police are dedicated to protecting the community and seeing justice served. It just takes some time."

We talk a little bit more about the logistics of what he'll need from us going forward, and how he intends to proceed on my behalf, before Oscar and I thank him and end the call. I'm feeling much less worried about the whole situation now. Part of that is Henry's conviction that the lawsuit won't go anywhere, but the rest is all Daddy.

I feel like I can face anything with him at my side.

Chapter Eighteen – Oscar

Even though he gave me a couple of personal days off to look after my boy, Rob still lets me take my scheduled week off as well. I resolve to buy that man the nicest bottle of bourbon I can find, because his understanding and support meant that I could look after my boy without worrying about the state of my job.

I never would have had that back home. In fact, my pops would have told me to tell my Boy to 'man the fuck up' or something equally as toxic. But Rob was just as concerned for Ryan's emotional and mental health as I was.

He's going to make a good Daddy for someone one day. Hell, if I was a switch, I'd totally be down for playing with him myself.

But I'm as Daddy as they come, I'm afraid. Plus, I don't think I'm Rob's type. And I'm also completely head over heels in love with Ryan.

I just hope the universe is kind to my boss and gives him a happy ending, too.

Because that's what I can see on the horizon for me and Rye: a happy ending. I know it's early days, and maybe this is further proof of my impulsive heart running ahead of logic and reason, but the magical few days spent in the cabin, being one hundred percent Daddy Dom and Boy, have left me on an incredible high.

We're back at Ryan's villa on the beach, and I can admit that I'm still in protective Daddy mode. Even though there's no hint of anxiety rolling off him now, I want to make sure my Boy remains happy and stress-free. Which is why I insist on bringing him a homemade lunch on Wednesday, when I know he's working in the clinic.

The waiting room is occupied by a couple of little old ladies with a cat carrier between them, and three empty seats on the opposite wall. There's a row of shelves on the side wall, containing a small selection of high-end dog and cat foods, and a display of flea and tick treatments. There's also a shelf containing pamphlets on a variety of topics: everything from signs of heartworm, to desexing, to puppy preschool.

I wanna attend puppy preschool!

Focus, Oz.

The reception desk, running along the other side wall, is currently empty, but I walk over and lean over the top of it, feeling the weight of the two ladies' stares on my back. I'm dressed in a pair of jeans and a t-shirt, so a lot of my ink is on display. I'm used to being judged for that, but the last thing I want is to cause any issues for Ryan in his clinic.

"Ring the bell, lovey," one of the ladies says, and I turn sideways, still resting on my elbow, to find her smiling at me.

I smile back, relaxing instantly. "Oh, no, I'm here on a social call, ma'am. I can wait."

Her companion's watery blue eyes widen when I speak and they both seem far more interested in me now.

"That's a pretty accent," says the first lady, nudging her companion, "bit like that show we used to watch back in the day. What was it, Beryl? Something Texas Something?"

With a long-suffering sigh tempered by an affectionate smile, Beryl says, "Walker: Texas Ranger, Shaz."

"That's the one!" Shaz —which I'm guessing is an Australian nickname for something only marginally longer— pats an age-spotted hand on Beryl's linen-covered thigh. "Thanks, love." Beryl looks back at me. "My memory's not what it used to be." She cocks her head. "You here for Sez?"

I know 'Sez' is Sarah's nickname. I haven't met Ryan's only colleague yet, but from all his stories, she sounds like a good friend to him. Nevertheless, I shake my head. "Here for Rye, actually. Uh, Doc Sharp." It feels strange using his professional title.

Beryl and Shaz exchange a look, raising white, wiry eyebrows and smirking at each other.

"You owe me five bucks," Shaz declares, and Beryl sighs. "Fine."

I decide I love the pair of them.

"Sorry for the wait," a much younger voice brings my attention to the young woman bustling down the short hallway beyond the reception desk. She's pretty, and looks to be somewhere in her mid-twenties, with blonde hair in a high ponytail and sparkling blue-green eyes. She's wearing powder pink scrubs, and her smile is contagious as she slides onto the chair behind the desk, her fingers poised over the keyboard for the computer. "How can I help?"

"No, love," Shaz cuts in from behind me, and I can hear the

smirk in her voice, "this hunk of a man is here to see Doc Sharp on a *personal* matter." I don't need to turn around to see her waggling her white eyebrows.

Sarah's eyes widen as her gaze swings back in my direction, having been focused on the woman behind me while she spoke. Her already contagious smile turns wicked as she takes me in, then in a blink she rounds the desk and wraps her arms around me, declaring, "You must be Oscar. It's so nice to finally meet you."

Chuckling, I hug her back, then release her. "It's nice to meet you, too." I lift the insulated bag containing the lunch I made. "I brought him lunch."

Sarah makes a show of swooning, pressing her hands to her chest. "Do you have a straight twin by any chance?"

"Unfortunately not."

"Pity," she sighs.

"Anyway," I redirect, sweeping my free hand towards my newfound friends, "I believe these lovely ladies are ahead of me."

"Oh, Boots won't mind waiting. He's here for his annual vaccinations," Beryl explains. "He hates vet visits."

As if prompted, a low, mournful yowl emanates from the cat carrier.

"Poor Bootsie," Beryl coos.

"Stop being a sook," Shaz directs towards the carrier.

Sarah laughs. "I think we should definitely get this over with for Boots," she says, then looks at me apologetically. "You don't mind waiting? You can come sit in the lunchroom while you do." She leans in conspiratorially, "We've got Harley, the cutest beagle puppy ever, in a kennel in there at the moment. He's a bit sad because he's just been desexed, so he could use some pats."

"I guess if I *have* to pet the cute puppy I will," I tell her, as though the task is a chore.

"Two secs." She turns to Beryl and Shaz. "Come on through."

The carrier yowls again as Shaz lifts it, wobbling a little precariously with its weight. "You're not getting any treats if you keep carrying on like that," she tells it.

"Don't listen to her," Beryl interjects, stooping to address the feline behind the bars, "I've got your back."

"You spoil him."

"I do not. I just show him affection."

They continue to bicker as Sarah leads them past me and down the hallway to the first of the doors on the right. Presumably, the treatment room, surgery, and kennel room/break room all back on to the reception area, one after the other, if the three evenly spaced doors are any indication.

"…this is why he's fat." Shaz's words are the last ones I hear as Sarah closes the door behind them then heads back over to me.

"I feel sorry for the staff at the retirement village with that pair," she tells me, but her tone is full of affection. Then she gives herself a shake and says, "Come on, this way," like there was any other option.

We reach the final door, and she gestures for me to place the insulated bag on the two-seat folding table positioned flush against the right wall of the room. The far wall has two rows of three caged kennels mounted against it, and the left side of the room is home to a small counter and sink, and a small fridge which has 'LUNCH' emblazoned over it in black sharpie.

"The, uh, the last staff kept mixing up the fridge in here with the one in surgery," Sarah explains with a roll of her eyes.

"Because it totally makes sense to put your sandwiches in with the meds in the sterile surgical room, doesn't it?"

"Wow," I shake my head. "Some people are…somethin' else."

"You said it." She moves over to the kennels and crouches down in front of the crate on the far right. "Hey, sweetie. You've got a visitor." The puppy inside whines and noses his way out, and I feel a pang of sympathy for the big, brown eyes overshadowed by the cone of shame.

"Aww, pupper," I crouch beside Sarah and reach out to scritch behind the pup's soft, floppy ears. "What did the mean doctor do to you? Did he take away your manhood?"

Sarah snorts. "Don't let Ryan hear you putting it that way. You'll get a lecture."

The idea of my sweet Boy lecturing me only makes me chuckle. "I'll take my chances."

The puppy gets impatient, bouncing his head under my hand as he whines again. I rub the top of his head with my fingertips. "Sorry, boy. Did I stop petting you?"

"Well, now that you understand the importance of your job here, I've got a few things to get organised. Shout out if you need anything." She pushes to her feet again but hesitates before she turns. "And, um, thank you for being there for Ryan last week. I don't know exactly what was going on, but it's obvious that you're good for him. I'm glad he's got you."

Before I can respond, she spins on her heel and leaves the room.

Harley whines and bumps my hand again.

"Sorry," I apologise again, "guess I need a bit more training at this job, huh?"

This is how Ryan finds me maybe fifteen or so minutes later, only I gave in to the burning of my thighs and sat my ass down on the linoleum floor a while ago. He snorts as he approaches but bends to press a kiss to the top of my head. "Oh, you're trapped now," he tells me. "He'll never forgive you if you stop patting him."

"Well, that's too bad, because there's another very good boy I want to spend time with."

Ryan groans. "That was a terrible joke." Even so, he gently guides Harley back into his crate and locks him in, seemingly unbothered by the pitiful cries from the puppy. Then he extends his hand and I grasp it, allowing him to help me up.

We wash our hands at the sink, and I pull our lunches out of the cooler bag when we take our seats at the table.

Harley seems to have settled down by the time we dig into our salads, which is good because my heart couldn't take the sad puppy sounds for much longer. I have no idea how Ryan does this for a living.

"So, you made quite the impression on Sharon and Beryl," Ryan tells me as we eat, and I can't help snickering.

"Sharon. Is that what 'Shaz' is short for? I'll never get over the way you Australians shorten everything."

"How is that any different to Oscar becoming Oz or Ozzy?"

I don't have a rebuttal. "…Touché."

With his lips twitching in the way that suggests he's trying to hide his amusement, Ryan spears a chunk of chicken and lettuce with his fork, then holds his forkful of food over his container. Apropos of nothing, he says, "I really do appreciate you, you know. Not just bringing me lunch, but taking care of me in general. I know it's a Daddy thing, but…I appreciate it."

Oh, my heart.

"I know, darlin'. I know."

* * *

"Oh, fuck," Ryan curses while I bend him over the arm of the couch in his living room, after having checked earlier that his hips and knees can tolerate the strain of this position. (With his thighs braced against the plush curve of the white leather, he assured me he'd be fine.) "Daddy, please—*Daddy!*"

His cries echo off the walls around us as I push the remote-controlled vibrating plug into his greedy hole, stopping my cum from leaking out of him.

My Boy has been so good for me all week (which, given his submissive, people-pleasing nature wasn't unexpected) and I'm in the middle of rewarding him with his most detested —and secretly craved— punishment.

Edging.

We took it a step further tonight, locking his perfect cock away in a cage before we even started, and it has been beyond satisfying watching him unravel.

I have reduced Ryan to a begging, sobbing, writhing mess, and I'm not planning on letting him come any time soon.

He whines when I step back and tell him to stand up.

I swat his ass, loving the way his flesh jiggles for the brief moment of impact, and he cries out again, rutting fruitlessly into the arm of the couch. Wearing the cage, he's not going to find any relief, but I scold him anyway.

"Nuh-uh, darlin'. You don't get to come until I say so." To punctuate my point, I tap the flared base of the large plug, knowing that it will send bursts of stimulation to his prostate. He pants and whines at the sensation.

Walking around the three-seater couch, I drop onto the middle seat, patting the spot beside me. "Let's watch some

TV."

He squirms but obeys, his posture stiff.

I lift my arm, beckoning, "Cuddle with me, baby."

Listing sideways, he tucks himself into my side and I reach for the television remote, selecting something at random. We sit for a couple of minutes in silence and, once I feel that he's relaxed, I pick up the other remote I placed on the side table earlier and press down on the button.

The buzz itself is muted beneath the dialogue from the TV show, and from being inside him, but Ryan jolts and yelps.

"*Nnngghh...*" The sound is half pleasure-half discomfort.

I rub his back and release the button.

When he starts to relax again, I press down on the button once more.

"Fuck!" he cries as his entire body jerks against mine. The cool metal of his chastity cage brushes my naked thigh. "I can't...Daddy, I can't...oh, God...Please..."

I release the button.

It takes a bit longer for him to settle this time, but as soon as I feel the tension leaving his shoulders, I set the vibrator off again.

"Daddy!" he sobs, turning his face into the crook of my neck, "Please! *Please!*"

I love seeing him like this. Babbling and straddling the lines between pleasure and pain. Desperate and uninhibited, showing me the ultimate vulnerability.

He rocks his caged cock against my thigh. "P-please. I need— I need to cum. I can't...Fuck, oh fuck...*help, Daddy...*"

The sharpness of his tone tells me that I've pushed him to his limits, and I know it's time to back off and give him his well-earned release.

After turning off the vibration for the last time, I wait for him to slump against me before I push him back. I snag the key for the cage from the side table and reach for his cock.

"Thank you," he murmurs deliriously as pretty tears slide down his cheeks. "Thank you, thank you, thank you."

I unlock the cage and carefully free his balls and dick from their stainless-steel confines, stroking the remaining lube from its application over his shaft. Unsurprisingly, it takes very little stimulation to bring him to full hardness, but I'm not completely ready for this to be over yet.

With my own dick straining again, despite having come inside him not all that long ago, I instruct, "You're not allowed to come yet. Not until I say you can," and wait for him to acknowledge me before I stand him up and bend him back over the arm of the couch.

He whimpers and starts to beg all over again as I tug the bulbous plug from his body to its widest point, then push it back inside him over and over again. His breathing is heavy and hitching, turning into choked-off gasps and sobs as he tries to hold back his orgasm under the force of my teasing.

Without warning, I tug the toy free and then drop to my knees to lick at his stretched hole. I can taste my own cum and remnants of the lube I used earlier, as well as the flavour that is uniquely Ryan, and my cock jumps in my hand, as if it's demanding to swap places with my tongue.

"I can't—Oz…Oscar…fuck! I…I…I…" Ryan has completely unravelled now, bouncing his hips backwards, encouraging me to fuck him with my tongue. "It's t-too much. Your tongue. Fuck. *Fuck.* I can't hold it. I'm going to come."

Tearing my mouth away, I bite the round flesh of his ass cheek, then insist, "You *can* hold it, sweetheart. You're Daddy's good boy."

He moans and his desperation is palpable. "I *can't*," he sounds almost broken, "I'm too close…Please, Daddy. I want to be good."

"Okay, honey, okay," I soothe him, surging back to my feet before grabbing is hips and sinking into him without further preamble.

"Yes!" he cries out, arching his back. "Oh my God, yes!"

I rear back and slam into him twice, and he shudders and sobs. "D-daddy…"

"You…*fuck*…" I hiss as he clamps around me, "You can come now, darlin'."

It only takes one more thrust of my hips for him to howl and stiffen as he erupts. I can't see his face, but I can hear his stuttered breaths and feel him trembling from the endorphin rush as he continues to paint the couch with his built-up release. I continue to fuck into him, letting the tightening of his body pull me over the edge again for the second time tonight.

I withdraw carefully and then help him up, dropping us down onto the couch, heedless of the cum we're spreading beneath us.

It's a leather couch. It will wipe clean.

Ryan is a mess, tear-streaked and boneless, and I cuddle him through the afterglow and come-down. I don't think he hit subspace tonight, but he's still blissed-out and thoroughly wrecked.

"You good?" I ask him, brushing back the strands of hair that have fallen over his sweaty forehead.

"Mmhmm," he agrees, then yawns widely. He snuggles even closer against me, rubbing his cheek into my shoulder. "I didn't know I needed that, but I did."

"Me too," I agree. "After the cabin" —I sigh, trying to work out how to phrase my feelings— "I just wanted to bring a bit more of that feeling home with us. Not that we don't already have that here, but…I don't know what I'm even trying to say."

He stills, then repeats, "Home?"

Shit.

Technically, I live on the station, but that's not where my heart is. Not anymore. But even though he knows that I love him, telling him that I feel like this is my home now is kind of huge, and also more than presumptuous. "Ryan, I—"

"I want this to be your home," he interrupts me. "I want this to be where you're happy. I want…" he swallows roughly and his voice cracks, "I want this to be our future. For—for as long we're both alive."

I can't help but think of his former husband, of the man he'd thought he'd get older and greyer with, and how much it means for him to have included me in the new, unplanned vision of his future where he'd once thought Maddox would be. They're big shoes to fill —I know it from the stories he's told me, and of how kind and welcoming Maddox's kids have been when I've spoken to them— and I'm determined to not take Ryan's trust that I'll fill it well for granted.

"I want that, too, darlin'." It would have scared me to admit as much, considering the mistake I'd made putting all my eggs in one lying, cheating basket not even a year ago. But there's no fear here now. Just the certainty that I am exactly where I should be. I bend towards him to brush my lips against his in a tender kiss, my voice barely a whisper when I repeat, "I want that, too."

Chapter Nineteen — Ryan

I wake on Saturday morning to an empty bed and the murmur of low voices drifting up the stairs and into my bedroom. Considering I'm not expecting anyone other than Oscar to be in my house —*our home*, I correct myself giddily— the fogginess of sleep evaporates instantly and I'm on high alert.

It's only the fact that I can hear the distinctive twang of Oscar's voice, calm and measured in whatever he's saying to whoever else is downstairs with him, which keeps me from leaping to conclusions about home intrusion or whatever. Nevertheless, I dress quickly, pulling on my discarded pj pants and a soft cotton t-shirt before hurrying down the stairs.

I stop as I hit the bottom step, blinking in surprise at the three people seated around the little dining table, all nursing steaming mugs of coffee. Oscar, I expected. But the other two?

"Papa!" Mak is up and out of her chair and flinging her arms around me before I can properly process what is going on. "You're finally awake. I thought Dad was the one who slept in.

You were always the early bird."

With my brain sluggish from only having just woken up, and still reeling from the surprise of seeing my step-kids sitting at my dining table so unexpectedly, my mouth engages before my filter does. "It's not my fault Daddy kept me up late."

Mortification kicks in at the same time Trev inhales his coffee and it erupts from his nose in a cacophony of splutters and choking sounds. Oscar passes him a couple of paper towels and sends me an amused look over the top of Mak's dark brown hair.

"Don't panic," he says calmly, already out of his own seat and moving around the table to stand at my side and rub my back. "Pretty sure one of us was going to slip up at some point. My money was on a couple of years down the line, mind you, but this just gets it over and done with nice and early."

My face feels like it's on fire. I cover my eyes with my hand, feeling Mak take a step away from me, ending our reunion hug. "Fucking hell," I curse myself. "Can we just forget I said that?"

"No," Mak says firmly, and I peek through a gap in my fingers to find her giving me a look so painfully reminiscent of Maddox that my heart hurts. I always did think she took after him more than her brother. Her eyes are soft with understanding and not even a hint of judgement, and her lips are curling upwards with a nearly invisible smile. "We're in your safe space, and unannounced at that. Plus, Dad would kick our arses if we even considered making you change who you are and what makes you happy. I…no," she looks over her shoulder to confirm with her brother, who nods, "*we* want you to be yourself around us."

My heart feels like it's going to hammer its way out of my chest, but Mak's words go a long way to bringing me down from an impending panic attack. "Even though he's your age? You…you don't think it's weird?"

"You warned us that he was younger," Trev says with a shrug. He balls up the napkins now that he's finished mopping up his accidental mess. "Granted, you didn't say how young, but age doesn't change whether a person is good or bad, and we can tell Oz is good for you."

"And the, um, the fact that I just…that I call him Daddy?"

Trev's lips stretch into a wide grin. "Is fucking adorable. You're never living it down, though."

I groan and turn to bury my face in the crook of Oscar's neck, and he pats my back consolingly, even while he chuckles. "You and Maddy raised damn good kids," he says, and it should be weird that he sounds so paternal about people only a few years younger than himself, but it doesn't. He's a Daddy, so the maturity is a natural setting for him in a way. However, there's a hint of melancholy when he adds, "I'd have given anything for parents like you guys."

"Maddy did most of the work before I even came onto the scene," I admit, and both my kids scramble to correct me almost immediately.

"Uh, no," Mak says, sounding affronted. "You came into our lives during our teens when we were at our most impressionable and annoying."

"You were never annoying," I tell her, and Trev scoffs.

"Yes, she was. Especially during her boy band era."

"Shut up," Mak shoots back at him.

He starts humming a One Direction song. She stomps around the table to smack his shoulder.

I'm instantly transported back in time, and it makes me want to laugh and cry all at once.

"What are you guys even doing here?" I ask instead, trying to stave off the tears.

They exchange slightly guilty looks and then Trev runs his hand through his sandy-blond hair and answers, "We were worried about you. With the lawsuit, and newly dating some younger guy, and living on the opposite side of the country…"

"I know we should've called first," Mak cuts in, "but you've always had an open-door policy, so we flew in overnight because we missed you and wanted to make sure you're okay." She points to the kitchen counter where a big Tupperware box is sitting and adds, "Mum even sent you a batch of her brownies."

I was never close to Mak and Trev's mother, Cynthia, but she was one hundred percent supportive of my relationship with her ex-husband. For as long as I've known her, she has travelled a lot for work, which was why Maddy had custody of the kids, but any time she was home, she would bake her signature brownies with the kids and send us batches when they'd come home. It's a bit of an emotional moment to realise that I haven't had any of her brownies since before Maddy died. Maybe even not since the kids were at uni.

"I'll have to send her a text to thank her." Then, registering the rest of Mak's explanation, I shake my head. "You're always welcome here, and you never have to ask whether you can come over."

"I mean," Trev looks between me and Oscar and smirks, "with this new dynamic, we probably should check you're not, uh, otherwise indisposed before we just turn up on your doorstep."

"A call from the airport would work," Oscar tells him. "One of us would come get you."

Trev shakes his head. "Nah, I always rent a car. I like being able to drive myself around."

"Fair enough," Oscar acknowledges.

"But, yeah, next time we'll call when we're on our way. Make sure you're decent or, at the very least, at home." His expression turns sheepish. "We're used to Papa being a homebody these days, but I'm guessing that might be different now."

"Eh," Oscar shrugs. "On the weekends I'm here, we do tend to stay close to home anyway."

I get a thrill at the reminder of last night's conversation. *Home.* This is our home. Together. Oscar gives me a squeeze, as though he's on the same page and thinking the same mushy thoughts.

"Oh, that's right. You're only here once every few weeks, right?" Mak asks, which prompts a conversation about Oscar's roster, and then his job, and soon enough we're all seated around the table eating Cynthia's brownies for breakfast, paired with fresh coffees and lots of laughter.

The kids don't bat an eye when I slip up and refer to Oscar as 'Daddy', and it's the best morning I think I've ever shared with my new boyfriend.

I can see this becoming our new normal, and I love it.

* * *

A couple of hours later, Henry calls.

"It's going to be fine," Oscar assures me when I stare at the phone in a panicked daze.

"Lawyers don't work Saturdays," I reply, and Trev snorts from where he's sprawled out on the couch reading a book on an app on his phone. How he can do that on such a small screen is beyond me.

"He knows I'm here," he says without even looking over. "So I can help with any legal jargon or offer my thoughts if need be."

Still paralysed in case it's bad news, I let Oscar pry my phone from my hand and watch as he slides his thumb across the screen to answer the call.

"Hi Henry," he greets cheerfully, "you're on speaker and the whole gang is here."

"Hello to the whole gang," Henry sounds jovial, which is a good sign, right? "Trevor, you owe me a dinner at Dan Arnold."

My eyes bulge. *A hatted restaurant? Henry has expensive tastes.*

"Fuck off," Trev calls back, eyes still on his screen. "The Cowboys had that game in the bag. Fucking Titans rigged it or something."

"Don't be a sore loser, mate," Henry chides, but he's laughing. "I'd hate to see you in court if this is the way you put a case forward."

Trev just raises his middle finger at the phone, which makes Oscar laugh. "You're not on video, man."

"Anyway," I prompt, my anxiety too high to properly enjoy the banter in the moment, "is everything okay with my case? Is there a problem? Do I need to come back to Brisbane?"

"Everything's fine," Henry assures me. "That's actually why I'm calling. I've been back and forth with the other guy's lawyer all week, but he's convinced his client to drop the case because they know they don't actually have one."

My knees go weak, and I drop into a chair at the dining table. "Really?" I croak.

"Really," Henry confirms.

Tearing up, I thank him effusively. "You have no idea how relieved I am."

"Oh, I think I have some idea," his tone is warm, even through the phone's tinny speaker. "But I told you the whole thing was bogus. It was just a waste of time and money on Old Mate's part. A stalling tactic against whatever criminal charges are heading his way. We could all see it: even his lawyer."

Mak and Oscar are sandwiching me between them, squeezing my shoulder and forearms while Trev sits up on the couch, paying attention now. "They *are* going to press charges?" he asks, all traces of his previous playfulness gone. He's in lawyer mode, gaze shrewd and lips set in a firm line.

"I believe so," Henry affirms. "Someone from the CIB will probably get in touch with you, Ryan, when they do. They'll explain the process from there better than I can — I'm not really across criminal proceedings."

"They'll want to hear your statements again," Trev says, looking between me and Oscar, "and they'll let you know when there's a court date and when you'll be required to testify—"

I stiffen and shake my head emphatically, already protesting that I don't want to sit in a court room reliving the assault.

"—which you might be able to give via video-link, seeing as you live out here now and have a business to run," Trevor continues gently.

I relax a little. That doesn't seem as daunting.

Trev looks at Oscar. "When they call, ask them to do a conference call and loop me in."

"We'll do that," Oscar affirms.

"So, it sounds like my job here is done," Henry says, reminding me that he's still on the line.

"Thank you so much," I repeat my earlier gratitude. "Send me your invoice and I'll pay it immediately."

"Nah, it's on me," he says, and I frown.

"I'm not usually one to tell someone how to run their business, but the best way to keep having a business is to accept payment for your services."

He laughs. "I'm doing well enough that I can afford to do a few phone calls for a friend for free."

"Henry…" I try, and he blows a raspberry down the line.

"Convince your son to honour his bet," he says, "and I'll consider us even."

"Oh, you're playing dirty," Trevor complains at the phone. However, he still sighs dramatically and adds, "I'll make reservations and let you know."

Oscar and Mak also thank Henry, and the call ends soon after. I can't believe how easily fixed the issue was after how stressed and scared I felt when I opened that letter last week. It feels anti-climactic somehow, not that I'm complaining that Henry was able to resolve it so quickly.

Knowing that there's still a criminal trial looming on the horizon still ties me up in knots, but the only impact that will really have on my life is knowing whether the bad Dom who assaulted me will face consequences or not. It's not going to have any sort of effect on my business, or my private life, or my relationships with people moving forward. I'm not going to go through months of defending myself or justifying why I made the report to begin with. Yes, I might need to answer uncomfortable questions about the club and the kinks I enjoy, but the people involved in the trial won't ever cross my path again. That's assuming it even goes to trial: it might even settle out of court if this guy wants to try for a lighter sentence.

All I know is that I was right for reporting him all those months ago. I didn't defame him, and he's not getting away with what he did to me. What he's probably done to other people, or what he might do again.

I have Oscar to thank for having my back then, and for continuing to support me now. He was the one who called Trevor and arranged Henry's help as well. Without Oscar, this all could have been a much bigger, scarier mess for me. Daddy or not, he's a good man. A good boyfriend. A good Dom.

"You okay?" he asks me softly, nuzzling his cheek against mine.

I close my eyes and breathe easily, feeling truly at peace for the first time in over a week, since the letter about the lawsuit first arrived.

"I'm better than okay," I answer. "And you made that happen."

"I mean—*ow!*" Trev rubs at his arm and glares at his sister who is rolling her eyes at him.

"Yes," I chuckle in his direction, "you helped, too. But if Oscar hadn't called you, I'd probably still be looking for the right lawyer to help me, assuming I would have pulled my head out of the sand at all."

"You don't give yourself enough credit, darlin'," Oscar says, and he wraps his strong arms around me and kisses the back of my neck. "You're stronger than you think."

"What he said," Mak seconds. "After Dad died, we all struggled. But you…you stayed strong for us." She gestures between herself and Trev. "You dealt with arranging the funeral, with selling the clinic, with making sure the wishes in his will were all met…you did it all and you never asked us for help, or accepted it when we offered."

"Because you're our kids," I fall back on the same argument I used over a year ago. "I was his husband. The adultier adult. It was my responsibility, not yours."

"Still dumb logic," she huffs, "but whatever, it's done. The point I'm making is that you did all of that because you're strong…only you've got a support system and it's okay to let others take over sometimes, too."

"Ah, fuck," I look up at the ceiling, blinking back tears at the gut punch from her words. She looks and sounds so much like Maddy that hearing her be so logical is bitter-sweet. "You're a pest," I accuse.

"I learned from the best," she teases back.

"Yeah," I agree, "your dad was a pain sometimes."

She picks up one of the cushions from the couch and lobs it at me. "I meant you, Papa."

"I know." And, because I'm mature, I poke my tongue out at her.

The serious mood starts to lift again.

"So, should we talk about what to expect when the police charge the guy?" Trevor asks, and I groan, shaking my head.

"Not today. I just want to enjoy this time with you guys before you fly back home. We haven't had proper family time since…"

Since Maddy died.

Oh, sure, I have spent time with the kids, but I was a shell of myself for most of the year following his death, and then I moved out here away from them.

"I can head out if you all want some time on your own," Oscar offers. He says it without a hint of resentment or upset, because he's just that sweet and understanding. But both kids and I deny him in unison: a chorus of horrified "fuck no"s.

"You're my Daddy," I tell him, without a trace of the embarrassment I felt when I first let it slip this morning. "And this is your home now, remember? You're a part of this family now."

"*Oh,*" Mak widens her pretty, hazel eyes and then grins evilly.

"Can *I* call you Daddy, too?" She rakes her gaze over Oscar with an exaggerated predatory glee, and I tug him close against me.

"Nope," I tell her. "Mine. Find your own."

"I'm so going to need therapy after this," Trev moans, then ducks as Mak attempts to smack him upside the head. "Papa, she's *so* violent."

"Only ever with you," she shrugs.

Trev sets his big, brown eyes on Oscar. "This is the insanity you're getting roped into. You prepared for this?"

"I'm the cowboy," Oscar says, "I do the roping." He looks at me with an expression so soft and full of love that it takes my breath away. "And I wouldn't want to be anywhere or with anyone else."

Chapter Twenty — Oscar

"You're going to tell me you're leaving the station, aren't you?" Rob asks after dinner on a Friday night nearly a year after I reconnected with Ryan.

I have loved every minute of working here. I have loved being a part of a found family of kinky queer people who love animals and the outdoors as much as I do. I have loved working on a ranch —station, *damn it*— with people who accept me for who I am, and who don't push their expectations on me (aside from expectations to keep up the good work, which are totally fair).

But, for all of that, I've loved being with Ryan even more.

When I first met him back in Brisbane, I felt a spark of connection. He was every single one of my weaknesses in a sexy, silver fox-shaped package. But the timing was all wrong, and I hadn't had confidence that I could be trusted to be the Daddy he deserved, not with my track record of impulsive, bad decisions.

Reconnecting with him changed that. I might not believe in

fate, but maybe the universe had been trying to tell me to take a chance. And if that beautiful Boy, with his tragic past, could be open to try letting someone new into his life, why couldn't I?

When we started this thing between us, I didn't allow myself to dream that I had found my happily ever after. Not after crashing and burning so badly when I first moved to Australia.

But over the past year, I'm convinced that my luck has turned.

Ryan and I love each other. He's my Boy and I'm his Daddy. He's also my partner, my lover, and my best friend. Our relationship is sturdy, built on a foundation of trust, communication, and hard work. We've had our share of arguments over the past months, as the newness and shininess of being in love settled into something more domestic, but we have always talked them out. Not once have we gone to bed angry with each other, and I'm not so arrogant that I can't admit when I'm wrong (which, as it turns out, is about eighty percent of the time).

For the first time in my adult life, I'm in a relationship of equal give and take. I'm with a man who grounds me and tempers my impulsive side, but who also encourages me to follow my dreams.

And that's why I'm sitting across from Rob in his homey living room, each of us nursing a tumbler of whiskey on ice.

My dreams involve spending more time with my Boy. I want to live with him more than a quarter of the time. I want to come home to him after each and every day of work. I can't do that while I'm here at Wombat Run.

"Yeah," I answer him with a great deal of sadness. "I love workin' here, Rob. I really do. But…"

"I get it," his smile is understanding, and it reaches his

sparkling eyes. "There'll always be a place for you here, but I don't think you'll need it."

"I appreciate that." He doesn't ask me what I'm going to do when I leave, and to be honest, I haven't figured it out entirely yet. But I've got an engagement ring burning a hole in my duffel bag, and every vision of my future from here has me spending my nights with Ryan in my arms.

"You're gonna invite us all to the wedding, I hope," Rob teases, and I choke a little on my drink.

"How'd you—?"

"Nothing gets by me here, Ozzy. You know that."

I haven't told a soul about my plans to propose. Not Dusty, not Jim, not even Rye's kids. I narrow my gaze, and Rob laughs. "I signed for your package, numb nuts. It didn't take a genius to put two and two together when I saw it was from a fancy-pants jeweller."

"Oh. Right." My cheeks burn and I duck my head. Clearing my throat as the moment of embarrassment passes, I ask, "Can I, uh, borrow the honeymoon cabin for a weekend? And maybe a couple of the horses?"

"Oh, I see how it is. You're quitting, but you still want the benefits of working here." Rob winks to let me know he's joking, not that I could have missed it from the giant smile on his face. "Of course you can."

"And, uh, if he says yes—"

"Which he will."

Ryan's got every right not to, and while it might hurt my pride, I'll understand if he doesn't ever want to marry again. It won't stop me from loving him or spending the rest of my life with him. "*If* he says yes," I repeat, "and if he likes the idea, can we maybe talk about hostin' the wedding here?"

Rob's eyes light up and get suspiciously shiny. He clears his throat. "You're pushing it, kid," he answers, but his voice is gruff with emotion, and that's all the answer I need right now.

* * *

A month later, I'm setting my plan into action. At this point, the news of my plans has filtered through the station like wildfire. I should have known it would: I work with a bunch of nosy Nellies and gossip queens. Still, the guys help me set up the cabin to match my vision, and they all stay out of sight when I take Ryan out on a sunset ride around the station.

He's not what I'd call a natural on a horse, but he knows how to handle himself in the saddle. In a nod to how we met, he's riding Jemima, while I'm on an appaloosa named Humpty. Ryan's bubbling, bright laughter at hearing the horse's name suggested I wasn't completely in on the joke, but I didn't mind. I just love seeing him happy and relaxed.

I take him over the paddocks and plains I've come to know like the back of my hand, bouncing gently in my saddle as we trot calmly over the patches of grass faded yellow from the sun. The sky is melting into deep orange and pink overhead, streaked with fluffy white clouds tinted almost purple around the edges. It's like being in a piece of art, humbling and surreal.

"I do love it out here," Ryan says, closing his eyes and breathing in the warm evening air as we bring the horses to a slow stroll over one of the hills overlooking the whole station. The countryside below us stretches on for what looks like forever; nothing but trees and paddocks and cattle as far as the eye can see.

There's a quiet stillness around us, broken only by the lowing of cattle and the hum of cicadas and crickets as they prepare for their evening concerts.

As I turn to watch my Boy, I'm almost struck speechless by how ethereal he looks, backlit by the setting sun in its rainbow of joyful colours. He has grown out his goatee into a full beard, and the silvery strands catch the oranges and pinks, making him glow. It reminds me of the evening we reunited, right here on the station. I'd thought he was lit up with beauty back then, too.

"I love you," I blurt, having lost track of the plan and all of my chill.

His eyes open, and even their grey-blue depths seem amplified by the majesty of the sky overhead. He smiles his usual sweet smile back at me. "I love you, too."

My heart hammers in my chest, and I know I'm not going to be able to wait any longer. I had a plan to take him back to the cabin after we stable the horses. The guys have laid out rose petals and have champagne chilling in an ice bucket. There's a nice dinner waiting in the oven, and a candelabra (unlit, because I wouldn't leave any kind of open flame unattended) on the dining table. I was going to get down on one knee and give Ryan a whole speech about how much he means to me, about how he has helped me to be the Daddy I've always dreamed of being, about how I can't imagine a future without him in it.

But this is the moment. Right here, right now. Surrounded by nothing but open sky, rolling red dirt and scrub pastures, and the soft huffing and chuffing of the horses we're riding.

I guide Humpty over to sidle up right next to Jemima, who sidesteps once but holds her place like the good horse she is, and I reach into the pocket of the light jacket I'm wearing.

My hand clenches tightly around the ring box, and I take a steadying breath before I bring it out and extend it towards him, popping it open as I ask without fanfare or my prepared flowery speech, "Will you marry me?"

Ryan's gaze flies from mine, to the ring, back to mine and I watch the emotions play out over his expressive, handsome face. Surprise, elation, love, trepidation…

"I…" he starts and stops, and my heart stutters with fear when sadness washes over his face. "I don't want you to go through what I did with Maddy."

With a lump in my throat and my heart beating at a million miles a minute, I shake my head. "Darlin', I already love you to the moon and back. Whether there are rings on our fingers or not, I'm with you to the very end, whatever that might be."

His Adam's apple bobs and tears slip from the corners of his eyes and trail down his cheeks, into his sexy as fuck glowing beard. "You arsehole," he complains and wipes angrily at his eyes with the back of one hand, the other still gripping Jemima's reins. "You're stuck with me, too."

"Is…that a yes?"

"It's a fuck yes, Daddy."

I whoop and holler, then apologise to the horses who stomp a little uneasily at the unexpected ruckus. Once they're settled again, I lean over and cup Ryan's jaw with the hand not holding out his ring, tugging him to my mouth for a long, deep, passionate kiss. When we part for air, I rest my forehead against his, repeating, "I love you, darlin'."

He sighs happily. "I love you, too, Daddy." He swaps the reins to his right hand and holds out his left. "Now, make it official already."

I snort. "You're still no good at bratting, honey."

He shrugs. "I've got a lifetime to practice now, don't I?"

Sweeter words have never been spoken.

"Bring it on, darlin'. I look forward to a lifetime of spanking that perfect ass of yours."

"You'd better put that in your vows."

I laugh, and we settle in to watch the sun lowering over the horizon. Eventually, we turn the horses around before we lose the last of the light and trot our way back to the stables with the promise of our future ahead of us.

When I met him, I had lost confidence in myself. He helped me rediscover it and has given me the happily ever after I thought was out of reach. No matter what happens from here, I hope I can be the husband, Daddy and Dom he deserves. I know I can't ever replace Maddy, and I don't want to. I just want Ryan to be happy and I think, together, we will be.

Forever.

Epilogue — Ryan

∝᧞᧞∝

"Well, don't you look hot as hell," Sez declares as she looks me up and down.

I snort a laugh and go back to fiddling with my bowtie in the mirror. *Why didn't I go with a normal neck tie?* "Aren't you supposed to say I'm handsome?"

"You're *so* far beyond handsome, boss-man," she tells me, striding over and batting my hands away from my neck. The same neck Daddy choked until I came in my damn pants last night.

Apparently, he wanted to keep to the tradition of not having sex the night before the wedding, but choking me to orgasm was somehow not sex? I didn't follow his logic, to be honest. Not that I was complaining at the time. I needed the session last night and he knew it. I guess he was feeling the pre-wedding jitters, too.

Sarah fiddles with my bow, tilting her head left and right as she perfects it. "There. All done." She turns me to face the mirror again and smiles at my reflection. "Hot as hell," she repeats. "Your cowboy Daddy isn't going to know what hit him."

I don't even react to her teasing anymore. She's become my best friend outside of Oscar, and she's just as accepting of my kinks as the kids and the guys on this station. But it doesn't stop her from giving me shit about it.

"He's going to look even hotter," I tell her with certainty.

I've never seen my soon-to-be husband in a suit. Not even in the lead up to our wedding. We went shopping separately, with Jim and Rob accompanying Oscar while Sarah came with me, leaving the clinic in Arthur's (the junior vet I eventually hired) hands for the day.

"You're both going to set the marquee on fire," she declares. "Should've gone for a less flammable setup."

"You're hilarious," I deadpan.

"Have you *seen* yourselves when you're together?" Sarah makes a show of fanning herself. "I'm telling you, set up an Only Fans. You'll be millionaires within weeks, and you'll get your man all to yourself — no sharing him with that hobby farm just outside Denham anymore."

"We're not making porn for your entertainment," I repeat a sentence I never thought I'd have to say, but which I have actually said more times than I can count over the course of the last eighteen months. "And he *likes* working at the farmstay place." Even if they're a lot more conservative than Wombat Run is. But it's a day job, he still gets to be out on a farm doing what he loves, and he always comes home to me. "He likes it a lot more than he'd enjoy having sex in front of a camera."

Although...

"I can leave," Trev says as he walks into the cabin and interrupts the naughty places my thoughts were about to travel.

Even though he throws his thumb over his shoulder and turns to leave, I don't miss the double take he gives Sarah.

Neither does she.

"Well, *hello*," she practically purrs, immediately losing interest in me for my son.

I'm immediately assaulted by visions of having her as my daughter-in-law, and I can't say I'm mad about it. But then I give myself a mental shake because Trev hasn't even said hi to the woman yet and I've just got marriage on the brain.

Because I'm getting married in, like, fifteen minutes.

My throat goes dry.

The last time I did this, I was closer to Oscar's age, and I would do it all over again without changing a thing…but the pain of losing Maddy still lingers on the periphery of my heart and soul, and the thought of me repeating history and causing that pain to Oscar still terrifies me.

But, like he said, with or without a ceremony, we're together until the end. The reality of life is that one of us will probably die before the other (unless there's some sort of horrible accident which takes us both out at the same time, but I don't want to imagine that). Life is unpredictable, and losses are inevitable. But love and the happiness we can share together far outweighs the sadness of whatever ending we have to face. In fact, it would be sadder not to love and enjoy a fulfilling life together.

God, these are depressing thoughts to be having on my wedding day.

"Dad would one hundred percent support this," Trev says as he comes to embrace me, and I lose the battle against my tears because, combined with the thoughts I've just been having, I needed to hear someone else say that. Not just someone, but Trev or Mak. My kids. *Maddy's* kids. "I know," Trev rubs my back. "It's bitter-sweet. I get it. But Oscar loves you. He worships you. Dad would want that for you. Not a life of loneliness because you're scared to get hurt by loss again."

"Get out of my head," I complain, hugging him even tighter.

"…and into my pants," I hear Sarah mutter under her breath, and it's so unexpected (and simultaneously *not*) that I burst into loud laughter.

Trev looks a little shell-shocked. I pat him on the shoulder, squeezing to impart my appreciation and love, and then I shrug. "Good luck with her, by the way."

I'd feel guiltier about foisting my oftentimes inappropriate friend off on my son if I didn't think he could hold his own with her, or that she wouldn't reel herself in if she thought for one second he was actually uncomfortable.

"Hey, so, are we ready to get this show on the road?" Mak asks, joining us. She's dressed like Sarah, in a summery dress that reminds me of the sunset here on the station, in splashes of yellow, orange and pink. She, like Sarah, is wearing ankle-high boots instead of heels, because it makes no sense to wear high heels on this terrain. Her dark hair is piled high on her head, and her makeup is light and natural. "Also, can I lodge a complaint with someone about *every* man on this station being gay? Like…is that even believable? How is there not one single bi or straight man out here?"

"Jim's bi…" I start, and she raises an eyebrow at me, planting her hands on her hips.

"Papa, he's only got eyes for the short, shy guy."

"Dusty."

"That's the one." She huffs. "So, I'll amend my complaint. Why aren't there any *eligible* men who like women out here, hmm?"

We leave the cabin and start the short walk down to the paddock where the marquee is set up. It looks idyllic, with the mostly-green field where the sheep live looking particularly lush under the bright blue sky.

"I didn't think you were looking for a relationship," I wonder aloud as we walk.

"A relationship, no. A fun time at a wedding, on the other hand…" she rolls her eyes as Trev gags dramatically.

"Children," I admonish lightly, and Sarah giggles.

"It's so weird hearing you try to be all…" she rolls her wrist, searching for the right word.

"Dominant?" Trev offers with a cheeky smirk. "Daddy-ish?"

Sarah bursts into a renewed peal of giggles and I groan, "Not *both* of you!"

"You introduced them," Mak tells me, as though I'd had any control over their short meeting only a few minutes ago, "so this is on you."

"You're right. Oscar and I should have eloped. I hear Vegas is fun any time of year."

Mak turns around and smacks my shoulder.

"Trev's right," I declare. "We really ought to do something about this violent streak of yours."

By the time we reach the marquee, my cheeks hurt from smiling and laughing. There's not even a hint of anxiety, and certainly no second-guessing my decision to marry Oscar.

The marquee is large and white, and between Sarah and Rob, the inside has been strung with fairy lights for the reception which will follow the ceremony. There are large floor vases containing sprays of native flowers —bright red Western Australian waratahs, yellow pincushions, orange banksias, billy buttons, wattles and bottle brushes— interspersed with eucalyptus leaves and other sturdy greenery, and the whole set up is just stunning.

However, I miss all of that detail as Oscar comes into view. We decided that neither of us would do a traditional aisle walk. Instead, we would enter the marquee from opposite sides and meet in the middle in front of the small gathering of family and friends. It's just us and the celebrant standing in front of everyone as my kids and Sarah take the seats reserved for them at the front of the room.

I was right: Oscar in a suit is something to behold. It appears to have been tailored to his body, the flawless matte black fabric stretched across his shoulders but tapering in neatly at his trim waist and hips. His tattoos peak out from his collar and over his exposed hands, and it makes me salivate.

His smile makes my already untrustworthy knees weak, but when he reaches out to take my hands in his, it steadies me. The warmth of his skin against mine, his calloused palms dry and his hold firm, grounds me to this moment.

This is my Daddy. My partner. My second chance at a happily ever after.

And I can't wait to get him out of that suit.

* * *

"I can't believe Dusty danced on the table," I laugh, flopping down on the mattress of the honeymoon cabin. It gives me a little thrill to realise that we're actually using it for our honeymoon this time. "Jim's face was priceless. Did you see him trying to coax Dusty back down?"

Oscar chuckles. "Those two will work out that they're head

over heels for each other one day." He comes to stand in front of me and extends his hand. "C'mon, darlin'. You're not sleeping in that suit."

The ceremony was beautiful. It was everything we asked for. Short and sweet, telling an abridged version of our story (there was no sense in getting the celebrant to go into the kinkier stuff) before we exchanged vows and rings and kisses. Then we hopped on horses (followed by the photographer in a ute) to have some spectacular wedding photos taken on the property before we headed back to the marquee to join everyone for the reception and party. It went so well, in fact, that Rob is considering advertising the station as a wedding venue now, in addition to the farmstay side of the business. I think it's a great idea. Then again, I'm hopped up on the endorphins from the day.

Even so, I'm also suddenly exhausted, and the idea of having to get up again now that I've sunk into the soft mattress is not at all appealing. "No," I whine. "Come cuddle, Daddy."

"I will. Once we're both out of our suits. C'mon." Oscar smirks. "Or do you want to give me a reason to spank you on our wedding night?"

"Do you need to have a reason?" The exhaustion is replaced by a burst of arousal. What a roller coaster of emotion!

"Get up, baby. Let me undress you. I've been wantin' nothin' but to get my hands on you since you walked into the marquee today." He palms his cock over the fabric of his suit pants. His shirt tails have already been tugged free, and his jacket is draped over one of the dining chairs, while mine is on the other. "I was half-hard for the whole ceremony."

Given that I felt the exact same way when I laid eyes on him, I find the energy to obey. We kiss as we undo each other's shirts and peel them from each other's bodies. Our mouths and tongues trail paths over every inch of freshly revealed skin.

It almost feels like it's our first time, despite our familiarity with each other's bodies now. But this is our first time as husbands, and by some silent agreement, we treat it with reverence.

When we're finally naked and our clothes are strewn around us on the floor, we move to the bed. It feels like Oscar's hands are everywhere, and I can't get enough of him. His touch, his scent, his body heat…everything about him drives me wild.

"I want…" I start, then steel myself for his inevitable protest, "Daddy, I want you to spank me while you fuck me on all fours. My knees can take it," I add. "I promise."

Since the beginning, he's been so careful about anything that might put pressure on my knees or hips, and I appreciate that, but there are times when I want to feel like I'm young again, and not inhibited by my body anymore. This is one of those times.

As expected, Oscar hesitates. "Why don't I spank you over my lap and then fuck you? Or I can bend you over the back of the couch again?"

It's a compromise we've gone with many times, but I miss the feeling of having the man I loved bracketing me over a mattress, of feeling the bed move under me as I'm pounded into from behind.

"Oscar," I pin him with a hard stare, hoping the seriousness of my tone imparts how much this means to me, "this is what I want."

"It's just that the last time you were on your knees, you could barely walk the next day, and not because of any sexy or fun reasons."

That had been the cause of one of our first real arguments. I'd pushed myself too far, had ignored the twinges in my joints, and Oscar had been beside himself that he hadn't realised and that I hadn't communicated properly. I understand why he doesn't want to start our marriage that way.

"I'll tell you if it gets too much this time. Please, Daddy? As my wedding present?"

"Jesus," he scrubs his hand over his face and sighs, "you know I'm powerless when you ask so sweetly. Fine. But," he holds up his index finger, "you tell me at the first sign of any joint pain. Understood?"

I nod and kiss him deeply in thanks, then grab the pillows for extra cushioning under my knees. I get myself into position and look over my shoulder, wiggling my butt in encouragement. "Come get me, Daddy."

He doesn't need to be asked twice.

Before I know it, he's lubed up and is sliding into me, and I put as much of my weight as possible onto my forearms which are braced on the mattress in front of me. Tears blur my vision at how right this feels. It might sound stupid, but it takes me back to my twenties and thirties, when I could fuck in any position I wanted, whenever I wanted. I needed to prove that I could still do this. That I could be everything for Oscar. That I could still be everything for myself.

I jerk forward at the first stinging, open-palmed slap to the flesh of my butt cheek. The sound of the smack is like a loud *crack* in the otherwise quiet room, accompanied only by our heaving breaths, moans and grunts. When the second one lands, I cry out, "Yes, Daddy, more!"

This is exactly what I wanted. His cock, thick and hard, stretching and filling me while he heats up my cheeks, making them sting even more every time he slams his hips forward. Euphoria builds inside me, from the pleasure and pain and the freedom that I'm feeling at being able to do this at all.

As the pain builds and my cries turn to gasps and sobs, I know I'm getting close to orgasm. I don't want to come. I want this to last for much longer. I want to feel Oscar inside me forever. I want my backside to be so tender that I can't sit for days without remembering tonight. I want—I want—

"Oh, fuck!" I cry out as he delivers another bruising smack to my abused flesh, then drives his cock home, bumping my prostate and making stars explode behind my eyelids. I'm so close, but with my own leaking, straining, aching dick untouched, I don't know if I'll go over the edge.

"I'm gonna come, darlin'," he warns me. "You feel too good around me. You're doin' such a good job, takin' my cock so deep."

At this angle, it does feel like he might be able to reach my tonsils. I shift my weight sideways, resting more on my left side with my face smushed into the mattress so I can slide my right hand underneath my raised hips.

The second I wrap my hand around my dick, I feel instant relief. I jerk myself in time with his next couple of thrusts, and delight in how ragged and raspy his breathing has turned.

Then, all of a sudden, he rears back and delivers three hard, resonating spanks to my stinging cheeks in rapid succession and I howl at both the pain and the orgasm it tears from me, covering my hand and the sheets beneath me with my release.

"Oh fuck," he pants, repeating the curse with the next three thrusts inside me, "oh fuck, oh fuck, oh *fuuuuck*."

I feel his cock pulsing and filling me up, and I slump all the way forward as he collapses over my back, his cock still twitching and spurting as he rides out the last of his orgasm. When he withdraws, I feel his cum dribbling out of me, and I groan when I feel him take two fingers, scooping up the mess and shoving it back inside me.

"Stay," he says, and the mattress shifts as he climbs off it. It shifts again and the cool, blunt tip of a plug pushes at my hole. "We're gonna keep this inside you for a bit," he says decidedly. "Your first gift from your new husband, darlin'."

My cock twitches valiantly as the plug settles in place, but there's no way it's going to get up again tonight. Still, I grin and allow myself to roll onto my back on the mattress, rescuing the pillows from the wet spot. "Happy wedding day to me," I say cheekily.

Oscar crawls over into the space between me and the edge of the mattress, also avoiding the wet spot in the middle. He kisses me softly, but I part my lips and encourage his tongue to tangle with mine for a long, loving kiss.

It's a kiss that symbolises so much for me. When he found me, I was only just putting myself back together. I was raw from heartbreak and grief, and he quite literally rescued me when I thought I was beyond saving. He taught me things about my kinky side which I hadn't known existed and showed me that my age really is nothing but a number in his eyes. He's my equal and my Daddy. My husband and my best friend.

When he pulls back, he nuzzles his nose against mine and whispers, "Happy wedding day to *us*."

With Oscar, I can see a future filled with love and companionship again, and I know he shares my vision.

Against all odds from that fateful night in Brisbane, we have healed each other, and this is only the beginning for us.

The End.

A Stable Daddy Playlist

I thought it might be fun to include some of the songs that give me Ryan and Oscar vibes. They might not match the plot exactly, but the feelings are there. The order below is probably the one that best matches the trajectory of their story, but I've also included the Spotify link for you, too. Fair warning, a lot of these are NSFW. Enjoy!

- Sex and Violence – Scissor Sisters
- Better Without You – Dixon Dallas
- Kissing Your Tattoos – Eli Lieb
- Touched By You – MNEK
- All My Life – Falling In Reverse feat. Jelly Roll
- Save A Horse (Ride A Cowboy) – Big & Rich
- Good Lookin' – Dixon Dallas
- Nothing Like A Cowboy – Cameron Hawthorne
- Tongue - MNEK
- Keep Riding Me – ur pretty
- MONTERO (Call Me By Your Name) – Lil Nas X
- I Guess That's Why They Call It The Blues – Elton John

- Something To Feel – Dixon Dallas
- Harder You Get – Scissor Sisters
- Fill Me Up – ur pretty
- That's What I Want – Lil Nas X
- Hold Each Other – A Great Big World feat. Futuristic

Find the Spotify link at:
https://annasparrows.com/stable-daddy-playlist/

About the Author

I've been writing* for as long as I can remember. I started with silly short stories as a kid, moved on to fanfiction in my teens, and then to publishing original fiction in my thirties.

I have been an avid reader of MM romance my whole life. Ask me about my beginnings with *Buffy* fanfic, haha! I wrote a sweet and kinky MM romance novel in 2022 and the reader response changed my life. From there, I knew I had found my niche.

And thus Anna Sparrows was born.

*All of my writing is 100% my own. No part of it is generated by Artificial Intelligence (AI) software of any kind. Yes, that means that it's sometimes flawed, but I'm okay with that.

You can connect with me on:

- https://annasparrows.com
- https://www.facebook.com/AnnaSparrowsAuthor
- https://www.instagram.com/annasparrows

Subscribe to my newsletter:

- https://annasparrows.com/newsletter-subscription

Also by Anna Sparrows

I write ridiculously sweet & steamy MM romance with guaranteed HEAs…and sometimes with a side of kink. My backlist can be found at annasparrows.com

Littles & Lace Series
The Littles & Lace series is an MM Age Play series, following a group of like-minded friends in the BDSM community. You'll find mild ABDL, light Pet Play, Femme Play and more here.

Book 1: Asher's Answer

Book 2: Matteo's Mettle

Book 3: Ted's Temerity

Book 4: Spencer's Satisfaction

Book 5: Chance's Choice

Book 6: Josh's Jackpot

Dads & Adages Series

Visit Australia's sunny Gold Coast where an assortment of single dads find love and even learn a few life lessons along the way.

Book 1: Where There's A Will

Book 2: You Don't Know Jack

Book 3: A Match Made In Evan (release TBA)

Shifters Sanctuary Series

In a world where alphas are thought to be extinct, a number of men are about to have their worlds rocked.

Book 1: His Alpha Unlocked

Book 2: His Prodigal Alpha

Book 3: His Unicorn Alpha (release TBA)